Claire,
Hope to read
your book next.

DEAD AQUARIUM

or

(i don't have the stamina for that kind of faith)

stories and novella

Caleb Michael Sarvis

Mastodon Publishing
Thoughts Made Real

Printed in the United States of America

First Edition
1 2 3 4 5 6 7 8 9

This book is a work of fiction. Any references to historical events, real people, or real places are used fictitiously. Other names, characters, places, and events are products of the author's imagination, and any resemblance to actual events or places or persons, living or dead, is entirely coincidental.

Cover art and design Ali Chica

Library of Congress Cataloging-in-Publication Data

ISBN 978-1-7320091-2-7
Library of Congress Control Number 2018956229

Mastodon Publishing
Thoughts Made Real
mastodonpublishing.com

For special discounted bulk purchases, please contact:
Mastodon Publishing sales@mastodonpublishing.com
Contact info@mastodonpublishing.com to book events, readings and author signings.

to my brother Jacob.
thanks for sticking around.

Contents

MUNDANE

Sinking Moments 13

An Unfaded Black 26

Goose Island 37

Unsolicited Independence 47

SUPRA-TERRESTRIAL

Scoop Carry Dump Repeat 53

Cages 66

Gastropod 70

Terra 76

(LOON)ACY

Emerson 85

SUBLIME

Bad Zeitgeist 155

Baby, It's Cold Outside 157

Vertical Leapland 162

The Matter of Dust 173

"The Past just left. Its remnants, I claim, are mostly fiction."
from "Doppelgänger, Poltergeist" by Denis Johnson

MUNDANE

Sinking Moments

Savannah uses an old Frisbee as a pillow. It's from her elementary days, something her father replaced rather than retrieved. The plastic is a faded green, somewhat akin to algae, and the face is dented in. It's uncomfortable, but better than the gravel of her roof shingles.

She fell asleep watching Venus in the west. Mars is there, too, to the left and faint, but Venus governs the navy stage. It's February, the planet at its brightest, shining like an impending doom that will never arrive. It doesn't twinkle, no. It reaches and it beckons. It pulls from the bicycle ridden home and onto the roof. Savannah watched it until it was all she saw and didn't move until something casual splashed in her pool, waking her up.

It feels like two, but dawn could be close, Savannah can't tell. Her phone died while she slept. Venus is gone, but Jupiter might be right around the corner. Something else splashes in the pool, quiet, like a weight discarded with intention. She scoots to the end of her roof, shingles scratching at the pockets of her jeans.

At the edge, peering into her backyard, she catches an older man sitting on the edge of her diving board, toes in the water. He wears a plain red hoodie and black shorts, a small box in his lap. His legs are dark and hairy. He pulls a Precious Moments doll from a box, tosses it into the pool, *kerplunk*. It sinks to the bottom, where Savannah snags a glimpse of three others. They rest inches apart, face up. Their eyes invite her down.

The man grabs another Precious Moments, but doesn't toss it. Instead, he holds it close to his face, and Savannah recognizes him. It's Mr. Boomla. He lives on the other side of the fence. He works for the post office, though he frequently publishes articles in the local Times. He might be Indian or Pakistani, and Savannah's ashamed she doesn't know for sure. In high school, they called her Pocahontas. Samoan, she'd correct, and they'd say, Seminole!

Mr. Boomla drops the porcelain doll into the water. Bubbles smaller than peas seem to catch it and lower it like a burial. The Precious Moments hits the floor of the pool, eyes up. Mr. Boomla coughs something ancient.

Savannah doesn't know why he sits on her diving board, nor does she feel compelled to ask him why. She repositions herself belly-first, and inches closer to the edge. Someone's lit a fireplace. The pool water smacks the tiled lips. The hum of the creeping filter accentuates the crickets she'd otherwise ignore.

Mr. Boomla pulls another Precious Moments from the box, then returns it. He flips the box upside down and fifteen or so more tiny statues splash into the pool. They sink as a single layer, a plane of disconnected glass, and find their place among the rest of the fallen. Mr. Boomla stands, tiptoes from the diving board to the grass, and disappears into Savannah's home.

Her parents left months ago. The death of Aunt Victoria, her mother's big sister, instilled a sense of urgency in their every-day, a coked-up rodent in their mortal awareness. Brooklynites, her parents teetered off in whispers of Napa Valley. Wine, the quiet, the color green. Victoria passed a couple months before Savannah's college graduation. Her parents left the day her diploma arrived in the mail. They booked the lodge for a week, and haven't returned in more than twenty, though she's stopped counting.

Her dates with Venus are an unpolished tradition. The summer between her sixth and seventh grade years, Savannah had to share her room with her Aunt Victoria. What this really meant was giving up her bed for the slow-leaking air mattress and falling asleep to the brazing serenade of Victoria's midnight phone call attempts. "Travis, it's Vicky, accept the charges," she'd say, but Travis routinely declined. Victoria only wanted change and affection. Travis wanted a clean conscience.

"You believe in other life out there?" she asked one of the few nights she let the phone be.

"If only because it's stayed far away from us," Savannah said.

"News says you can see Venus tonight. Look west around nine o'clock, it'll be the bright one among the specks." Aunt Victoria's voice slithered with defensive confidence, a bravado convincing enough for a twelve-year-old girl.

With the help of her aunt, Savannah found her way through the window and onto the roof. She found the planet immediately, and the quiet of outdoor suburbia, the hypnosis of galactic twinkle, lowered her to the only peaceful sleep that summer.

Savannah uses the gutter to lower herself into her bedroom window.

Clothing coats her floor. Partially filled glasses sit on furniture, fingerprints present in the moonlight. The screech of a chair dragging across the wooden floor sounds from downstairs. Mr. Boomla doesn't know she's there. She's sure of this, and she isn't afraid otherwise. But what is he doing in her home? She ditches the jeans and slides on a pair of Soffes. She unclasps her bra and pulls it through her shirt. In the dark, she studies her silhouette in the mirror.

The carpet of her hallway is plush enough to hide Savannah's steps. She sidles from her room towards the staircase and catches Mr. Boomla standing on a dining chair, gazing at the picture frames on the vaulted wall near the television. His eyes seem fixed to the top, a large picture of her parents outside Barclays Center. Savannah feels somewhat disappointed, assuming Mr. Boomla's presence was the result of a secret affection for her. After all, she is attractive enough. Young, tan, and tight. She understands that when her hair falls a certain way, it can alter a man's step, drop weight in the other foot. Just below the picture of her parents is one of her, donning a cropped sweater and thin jeans in front of the World Trade Center memorial fountains, a spring vacation. Mr. Boomla doesn't appear the least bit interested. He continues to gaze at the picture of her parents.

The lights of the pool wave through the sliding glass door. The moon peeks behind it.

Mr. Boomla pulls the picture from the wall, steps from the chair. He sets it on the loveseat nearby and pulls the rest of the frames as well. Soon the wall is bare, save for the protruding screws and crumbs of dry wall striping inches below.

Savannah descends the staircase.

Mr. Boomla has been her neighbor since her days of plastic roller skates and Fisher Price wagons. Before her Frisbees found the roof they'd float over the fence into his yard. The knocks on his door carried an extra echo.

"Again?" he'd say, eyes draped with impatience. He couldn't have been more than thirty-five in those days but sagging glasses and cigarillo balanced between his lips, Mr. Boomla occupied the space of an aged generation. He never let her inside and would disappear for minutes, an eternity for a nine-year-old. Savannah remembers the small glass tables on his porch, ash trays full. Once, she found herself digging through the closest one, enthralled by a dead lizard, cigar butt in its mouth. A cause or a dressing, she couldn't be sure. The front door swung open before she could touch it. The green disc dangled from a brown hand. "Why don't you try throwing it the other direction?"

Eventually the Frisbee found the roof.

Occasionally, he'd have evening parties. A lively saxophone, heavy cigar smoke, the clanking of glass. Savannah used to peek between the planks of their fence, absorbing and desiring adulthood while her parents partook in a night swim. Men and women laughed for no reason, blew smoke at the stars, rested fingertips on elbows. Once, she spotted Mr. Boomla kissing a small, dark-haired woman near the palm tree on the side of his house, only for another man to come out and say it was time to go. The woman met the man at the sliding glass door and Mr. Boomla remained hidden in the shadows behind the palm.

"Where's Rob?" the man asked.

"Must be in the bathroom," she said.

After they left, Mr. Boomla lingered in his backyard alone, sipping from a clear, short glass, the butt of a cigar glowing from his loose hand.

At the foot of the stairs, Savannah is reminded of that moment. Mr. Boomla, picture frame in hand, looks shamed again. Mouth slack, eyes round, hungover epiphany.

"What are you doing here?" he says, accent thinner than in the days of her youth.

"I live here. I've always lived here."

"I haven't seen anyone for months. I thought this home was foreclosed on."

"Only abandoned."

Savannah realizes she hasn't been in her backyard in quite some time, since before her parents left. The only lights she uses are her bedroom and bathroom, and the windows for each are on the side of the house, out of Mr. Boomla's view. He had every reason to believe the house was empty.

Mr. Boomla sets the frame with the rest. The wall is bare.

"What are you doing?"

"I'm sorry. I really thought nobody was here," he says.

She nods at the wall. "The pictures."

Mr. Boomla steps to his right and presses his palms flat against the garnet paint. He rubs a screw with each pad of the thumb. "I had two ideas. I could smash, or I could paint. I could also replace, I suppose."

Savannah steps to the love seat, grabs the picture of her parents. "Mom and Dad wouldn't approve. What's wrong with your own walls?"

Mr. Boomla drops his head and walks into the kitchen. "They are beyond alterations." He opens cabinets, inspects the fridge. "Where does your family keep the alcohol?"

"It was gone days after they left. Never grabbed anymore." A lie. She keeps it in her bedroom. She thinks of Mr. Boomla's walls, punctured, stained, and hiding rot. Perhaps his carpet is peppered with drywall. She imagines his insides a maze of soggy splinters, his heart a mine of mites.

Savannah watches him bounce his head into a couple more cabinets, before pulling a case of canned Yoo-hoo from the pantry. "This will do." He carries the case from the kitchen to the couch. There's something inhuman in the way he walks. An animalistic apathy to the world around him. Here he is, in a house he doesn't belong, content to sip Yoo-hoo and study photographs of a family that isn't his.

Mr. Boomla snaps a can open, gulps a bit of it down, and makes a face. "Ugh," he says and drinks some more. He doesn't have bags under his eyes, no, but shallow caverns. Little impressions where the skin looks thinner, capillaries visible in the faintest of light. Savannah can see that his hoodie is stained, corners crusted where neglect took root.

"I can't say I'm comfortable with this. It's the middle of the night." She says this but is relieved when he doesn't move. She wants to play "coy," a word she can't quite define. She's jonesing for his gaze.

"Have a Yoo-hoo. Let me tell you about my wife." Mr. Boomla holds a can in her direction.

The parties continued less frequently as she grew older. Savannah transitioned from peeking between fence posts to watching from the shadows of her roof. During her sophomore year, she smoked pot from a dirty bowl and watched the same woman visit often. She and Mr. Boomla would sip wine on his porch, their expressions shaped by the light of the fire pit. This is where Savannah learned romance, something she didn't know before but realizes now.

The woman's visits grew from every few weeks to two nights a week. Savannah grew to recognize her presence prior to her arrival. Wine on the porch, mosquito candles lit, low volume jazz teetering from inside the house. Sometimes Mr. Boomla prepared too early in advance and would sip from a separate bottle of wine, only to replace it upon the woman's arrival.

They'd smoke, they'd laugh, and after a while, as Savannah returned to her bedroom window, the woman would climb into Mr. Boomla's lap, weave her fingers through his thinning hair.

Her second semester of college, Savannah sipped a glass of water and MDMA, awaited Venus, and caught Mr. Boomla sipping his glass of red near a mosquito candle. It was one of his more anxious nights, but halfway through his second pour, when the woman would usually arrive, Mr. Boomla remained alone. He finished his drink, weighed the bottle in his hand, set the glass down, and disappeared inside.

Half an hour later, as Savannah's cocktail hit, pool water lapping softer than usual, Mr. Boomla returned outside and collected the glasses he'd set for the night. He poured the rest of the open bottle in his own glass. His brow furrowed, sweater a pure red, and wine similarly bright. His disappointment was made palpable by the drugs, and in that touch Mr. Boomla was momentarily beautiful. Something within Savannah reached for him, and he faded into the house.

Venus pinched the night sky. Soon Savannah forgot Mr. Boomla, and for the evening, herself.

Mr. Boomla never married the woman because she never divorced her husband. It's not the Catholic way.

"But she is my wife. I don't need a document to validate that fact," he says. A sensitivity glazes his eyes, some kind of aloof alertness. He lies on the couch, feet on the armrest, empty can on his chest. "We may not be present with each other, but our belonging is infinite."

Behind his head, above his own home, the moon is outrageous. A crawling inflation, a balloon of looming plaster. What looks like a shooting star flies above it but is too quick for any confirmation.

Savannah stands. She catches the moon in the surface of her pool. "When was the last time you spoke to her?"

"We speak every day, in our own way."

"Then why drown the Precious Moments?"

Mr. Boomla rests a new Yoo-hoo on his chest and taps the side with a fingernail. Something raw in the garbage reeks. "It was petty. I've called twenty-seven times without a response."

"That's too many times."

"Well, ah…" He waves at a pest Savannah can't see. He scratches at a thick layer of facial hair.

"Do you want them back?" She holds the picture of her parents in her hands. Mr. Boomla's presence is still unsettling, but she's easing into the adventure of it. A gram of marijuana sits in the drawer of the coffee table. Half a handle of tequila rests beneath her bed. She doesn't feel compelled to chase either of them.

"I don't really know," Mr. Boomla says. He finishes the Yoo-hoo.

Savannah opens the sliding glass door. Winter air slices into her lungs. She's ignored the last week's worth of her parent's calls. Always in the evening, in the middle of a movie or a drink or a song. She wonders if her parents feel like Mr. Boomla, dislodged from orbit by neglect.

"Did you know that two black holes, massive fuckers, are set to collide in another galaxy?" It's something she read weeks ago, an internet rabbit hole. Mr. Boomla is silent, so she continues. "It's not supposed to happen for one hundred thousand years, which is really no time at all in the grand scheme of things, and when it does, the energy it releases is supposed to have profound effects on the rest of the universe." Savannah steps out onto her back patio. Walks towards the pool. She sits on the edge. "And when you think about human existence, the way we've evolved, progressed, in the last two hundred thousand years… it's impossible to imagine where we'll be when that energy is released." She dips her toes in the water. Goosebumps spread across her exposed legs. "That is if we don't destroy ourselves first."

She hopes this makes him feel small, that humanity is hardly significant.

Mr. Boomla hasn't followed her outside. From the backyard, her skin blued by pool lights, Savannah can no longer see him. Another shooting star scratches the sky, this time she's sure. She pulls her shirt over her head; her breasts breathe in exposure.

She dives into the pool.

Aunt Victoria's death was an unspoken relief on the rest of the family, especially Savannah's mother. Most families have one; those were the consolation words of her father every time a new police station called their home. Shoplifting, unpaid parking tickets, selling cigarettes to neighborhood middle schoolers—Victoria held a bucket list of petty crime, tenacity her lone good trait. Of course, Savannah's mother was devastated by the news, but only momentarily. Through the initial tears, the sighs of disbelief, Savannah noticed a few wrinkles fade away. The hard knot of her mother's tight jaw melted into a rounded softness, and while her eyes glued themselves to the horizon, tidal lines crashing as she forced the tears out, Savannah caught a change in her breath. Deep through the nose, crash onto the shore. When her father held her mother following the funeral, he almost looked grateful.

Savannah was happy for her parents when they left. She'd never known them to vacation, and an empty house was too appetizing to acknowledge any real concern. When they extended it one week, she was admittedly disappointed to prolong the home-cooked meals. By the time they were gone a month, she'd already felt herself passing the days with movies and alcohol, no real curiosity in her gut. The details of the wallpaper grew bold. The creaks of a settling house became familiar. She'd awake to idle television screens and fall asleep trying to remember her week. When she imagined a house to herself, it filled itself with friends, but now Savannah couldn't bring herself to interrupt the peace.

She stopped answering her parents' phone calls because she had nothing to say, which wasn't their fault, but it felt better to pretend.

A few weeks ago, Savannah invited a boy over. His name was Max, and he was an old high school classmate she'd been messaging online. He wore jeans a size small, combed his blond hair to the right, and inhaled too much on his first hit from the bowl.

Max messaged her first, complimenting the series of poolside photos she'd uploaded. The photos were a year old, done by an old friend to make an ex-boyfriend jealous, and unpublished prior to now. Max mentioned wanting to see the pool in person, asking if she'd wear the bikini from the photos. It was late January, and Savannah told him she was free the next day.

As she straightened her hair, her eyes looked to have shrunk. She didn't spend much time studying her reflection these days, and after swooping liner across her eyelids and stroking mascara across her lashes, her eyes still felt a little lifeless. She worried Max might think she was disinterested. Savannah considered canceling the invitation, unsure why she had extended it in the first place. Her abdomen fluttered as she listened to the silence of the house. Shame. Before she could establish the merit of their plans, her phone buzzed with a message. *On my way*, it said.

They smoked two bowls upstairs, neither mentioning the pool or even the bikini. On her bed, Savannah pulled at Max's cheeks, complimented his teeth. He ran his fingers through strands of her hair, eyes on her neck. For a while, nobody broke the moment. He slid from her bed onto the floor. He laughed at the Shawn Hunter poster she'd tacked above her dresser. She followed him down. They smoked a little bit more. Relaxed. When she nibbled his dangling earlobe and caressed the inside of his thigh, he pulled away and turned his laughs towards her.

"I'm sorry," he said. "This was what I had in mind, for sure."

"But what?"

"You're just too much like a sad puppy." He laughed some more. "You get it."

She pulled herself onto the bed, lay on her side and stared through her window. She understood, but she couldn't help it. When Max walked through her door, she felt as though she'd been fasting, and all she wanted was to be fed. When she peeked over her shoulder to see if he was watching her, he'd already left.

Savannah doesn't know how long she's been underwater. Her bones hollow with cold, her fingertips shrink into raisins. She's cross-legged, butt on the bottom. Precious Moments surround her.

She's only faintly familiar with the dolls, porcelain figures with engorged eyes, frozen in the instant before weeping. Most are dressed in long white robes; some even have wings. Many of them press their hands together in prayer. She understands they are a collector's cult of another generation. Beanie Babies for the religious. The archaic cousin of LaserDiscs. Her parents are Christian, she thinks, if only out of habit, but the concept of religious décor is strange. It doesn't translate, especially now at the bottom of the pool.

One of the Precious Moments bounces towards her, seemingly deliberate. It's a small girl, clutching an even smaller puppy to her chest. It leans one way, then the next, and as it reaches Savannah's ankles, she sees it's Aunt Victoria. Yes, the dark hair unmistakable, the mouth turned downward despite the artist's painted smile. Or is it Mr. Boomla's wife? And Savannah understands what he meant earlier. She believes in their infinite. This is tangible aura; she can feel it in her lungs. Mr. Boomla's wife is squeezing the life out the puppy; then she floats onto her back.

Savannah does the same, sinking softly, landing and bouncing on the rough floor of the pool. This is relief.

Through the surface, in a jagged patch of sky where everything is darkest, shooting stars zoom in dozens. The silent finale, all flash and no boom, until it's all erased by bubbles. She floats—a force she doesn't feel lifts her to the surface. The bubbles and the stars are one. The patch of deep black grows. She breaks.

Mr. Boomla boils water while Savannah huddles in a blanket on the couch. The Precious Moments sit on a towel atop her coffee table. He must have fished them out after laying her down. He wears one of her father's t-shirts, a pair of his sweatpants. The little hair he has sticks high like an after-nap. He drinks another Yoo-hoo, whistles a song she's heard before but can't name.

"What is that?" she says.

"With God on Our Side," he says. "Dylan."

"Are you Hindu?"

"Parsi." Mr. Boomla pours the boiled water into mugs, drops a tea bag in each. "But the sentiment is unconditional."

"I don't understand the dolls."

Mr. Boomla sets the mugs next to the Precious Moments. He sinks into the loveseat. "Her husband wouldn't allow them in the house. Said they churched enough. I told her she could keep as many as she liked at my place."

Savannah reaches for the small girl holding the puppy and no longer finds any familiarity in it. The eyes are one with the rest of the figurines, the hair flat and lifeless.

"These are really fucking creepy," she says.

Mr. Boomla laughs, pulls one close to his own face. "Sometimes I'm not sure if she came over for the wine, for me, or for these. But most of the time I don't care. I'm just happy she showed." His face falls when he says this, eyes large like the statue he holds. "It's hard to begin again over there."

They are quiet for a while, Savannah conscious of her nakedness. Mr. Boomla seems unconcerned. The blanket is reassuring against her soft skin, but she's displaced by his indifference. She readjusts the blanket so a patch of skin below her neck is exposed, a crooked trail of suggestion. She runs her fingers through her hair.

Mr. Boomla leans back, shuts his eyes. "Was that a suicide attempt? I've never seen one, so I can't say for sure." He isn't charged by the question, the tone of his voice level. "A friend in high school died in a car accident following a breakup. It always seemed a little curious."

"You think he did it on purpose?"

"No one found a note or anything. But, yeah, I imagine he did."

Savannah tries to imagine herself behind the wheel of a car, sight filtered, chest aflame. A heavy foot is an easy decision, the jerk of a wheel another.

"Suicide seems too conscious for anything I'd do," she says. "I prefer indecision."

"It does seem recent days tumble like dreams." Mr. Boomla opens his eyes. They settle on Savannah, her exposed skin. The way they linger is shameless, then they shut again.

"There are plenty reasons to forget her," Savannah says. "Plenty of ways."

"I know to be young is to be reckless, but you should really be careful. People die holding their breath like that," he says.

Savannah returns the blanket so that it covers her chest.

Then he's in the kitchen, pulling the last few Yoo-hoos from the box. He returns to the living room and stuffs the Precious Moments inside.

Savannah coughs, and Mr. Boomla asks if she's okay. She nods, and he finishes packing the figurines. He stuffs his feet into a pair of

Timberlands. Soon he's stepping past the sliding glass door, around the pool, and calling for her to follow him.

Mr. Boomla pushes himself on top and over their dividing fence. When he's on the other side he asks for the box and she places it into his waiting hands. He takes the box, and she sees nothing of him.

"When your parents return home, come over for a jazz party," he says. "You're an adult now, right?"

She hears the crunch of dead grass beneath a boot.

"It wasn't a suicide attempt," she says.

No response.

Savannah showers the chlorine out her hair, redresses in dry clothing. Venus is gone and twenty or so hours from return, but she climbs onto her roof anyway, mug of tea in hand. She looks to the opposite horizon, where a layer of orange divides sky and landscape. Just above it is Jupiter, not as bright as Venus but equally reliable. The dew of overnight smells like fresh linen, and Mr. Boomla opens the blinds of his bedroom window.

The morning still dark, Mr. Boomla's lamp creates a clear view into the room. He sets a small suitcase onto his bed and stuffs it with balled t-shirts and underwear. He does this hurriedly, moving the Precious Moments from the Yoo-hoo box to spaces between the clothing. When he's finished, he zips the luggage and turns off his light.

Savannah finishes her tea and hears the engine of a small car start up. It rumbles in place for a few minutes and moves a little farther away before traveling down a street on the other side of the house. She doesn't see anything except for her own curiosity waving with the palmettos and wonders if this is a delivery or the beginning of a chase.

An Unfaded Black

Grandpa Sly's tooth fell out. The left incisor, Miles thought, whichever was the vampire one. It fell out of his mouth and into his coffee as he explained clichés to Miles. While Miles didn't need the help, he'd been assigned guardian duty by his mother. They sat at the low wooden table, a corner between them. Grandpa Sly held the essay flat on the table, and drooped his head forward so he could make out the words, following the lines as if they were Braille. "Dark as night," he was saying, and coffee splashed onto the line about the vast emptiness of outer space.

Miles stared at the newborn space in his grandpa's mouth.

"Try something like dark as wet coffee grounds instead," he said, and took another sip from his mug. "Or dark as the essence of a life looked back on."

"Dark as your hair?"

"Nobody knows who I am. I've no hair left."

Grandpa Sly smoked cigarettes well before he shot his sixteen-year-old son Bobby dead in 1973, but Miles' mother said he was up to three packs a day after that. He'd cut it down since starting chemotherapy but still smoked a handful daily.

Years of D.A.R.E. and Tobacco Free campaigns taught Miles a lot about the consequences of smoking cigarettes, but it was awareness akin to walking on the moon. He believed it existed, but not within his realm of experience. At least, not until Grandpa Sly moved in with them to die. He might have avoided the brunt of it had it not been for his poor history grade and the convenience of his grandpa having been a successful copywriter in 1969.

"All of it's online," he told his mother.

"Yes, but your grandfather is not," she said.

Of course he wasn't online! When Miles told his grandpa he'd like a cell phone for his birthday, his grandpa scoffed at the idea and said, "You need to learn how to be alone." But that was the point, Miles had thought. With a cell phone, the internet, he could always be alone. Instead, he was stuck at the dining room table with "Dying Sly," as he called himself, learning about clichés instead of Neil Armstrong and Buzz Aldrin.

Miles searched the rest of his paper for other pieces of "recycled nonsense" while his Grandpa Sly, mouth open, stared through the doorway into the family room where a large flat-screen television was mounted on the wall. Saliva bridged his lips like the webs in their attic. Though the television was muted, Miles recognized the orange scheme and the intrusive megaphone of the Tobacco Free campaign. His grandpa furrowed his brow; his eyes glossed in a reminiscence Miles was learning to recognize. A thin hose rested atop his lip, doing the work his lungs couldn't these days. "I used to be the best. I could sell anything. Now they want to destroy my life's work," Sly said.

"Your ad work?"

"Don't let anyone ruin you, Bobby."

"I'm Miles, Grandpa. Bobby died."

"Not you, dammit. Him!"

Miles looked to the family room but saw nothing and returned his eyes to the space where his grandpa's tooth used to be. Maybe the tooth had been a valve and now he was slowly losing his mind, too.

Grandpa Sly shot Bobby dead because he'd just taken a small hatchet to his sister's forearm. Miles's mother told him that her father's biggest regret had always been raising his children in Brooklyn, rather than getting them out when his wife was still alive. "He spoke fondly of the Poconos," she said to him, trailing at the end as if she didn't believe it herself.

His mother was too young and shocked to remember the details, other than Grandpa Sly telling her the doctors found a "landfill of dope" in his system. They amputated the front of her arm, right above the elbow, and when she was in a particularly sour mood, Miles' mother would scold him without her prosthetic, pointing her doughy stump for emphasis. Only recently had Miles considered what kind of terror she might be holding in. On a couple of occasions he heard her awake from a bad dream, repeating "No, no" forcefully before settling into the night.

"Black as a nightmare?" Miles asked his grandpa, snapping him to attention. He didn't want his grandpa to die before his mother returned home. He wasn't ready for that kind of responsibility.

"What?" Grandpa Sly swung around and knocked the mug over. Coffee spilled across the table, covering the history paper and into the middle of the puddle rolled the stained, dead tooth. The top half, once rooted in the gum, faced Miles and briefly swallowed his sight.

His grandpa pushed himself away from the table. "It was shit. Nobody would've bought it anyway."

Miles wanted to tell him it was a school paper and not a piece of merchandise. This was a kitchen in suburban Maryland and not his office in 1960s Manhattan. He wanted to go up to his room, open his laptop and find everything he needed in a matter of seconds because this was 2017 and why couldn't everyone just let it be 2017?

Grandpa Sly shuffled into the family room, dragging his oxygen behind him. Miles grabbed the roll of paper towels from the kitchen and watched the coffee spread across the white, a slow and irreversible growth. When everything was wiped clean and his paper in the trash, he grabbed his grandpa's tooth, dropped it in a plastic bag and stuck it to the fridge with the magnet shaped like the Empire State building. At first glance, it looked like a souvenir awaiting the Tooth Fairy's arrival, but as he hung it, Miles knew if anyone came for it, they'd be taking Sly with them. Maybe he and Bobby would find each other. Maybe Bobby would be cloaked, wound still fresh, wielding a scythe. *Black as the reaper's face?*

"Bring me my glass," his grandpa called from the family room. "Two cubes. Not three."

Miles grabbed the short rounded glass, the only one Sly would drink out of, dropped two ice cubes and brought it into the family room.

"Bourbon."

"It's early. Mom wouldn't like this."

"Abigail? What does she know? She knows better, that's what."

Exactly, Miles thought. He glanced at their front door. His mother would be home with groceries soon enough. He wondered if his grandpa would drink quickly as he walked into the kitchen. Miles grabbed the only dark bottle from the shelf and filled his grandpa's glass.

"Bobby, reach under that cushion there and grab the small carton."

Miles turned to correct him but his grandpa wasn't looking at him. He set the glass on the end table. "Which cushion?"

"No, I want *him* to get it."

"I don't think he can."

"Fine, the middle one." He waved at the couch across the family room. "But I don't understand why he's acting like this."

Miles didn't believe in ghosts, but walking across the family room, he was on guard and didn't know what for. He was wary of what he couldn't see, of what he couldn't feel, the weight of a whispering presence. Faces of strangers flashed from the television. *Black as a tarred lung?* Cicadas roared as one outside of the window. He lifted the middle cushion of the couch, grabbed the small cigarette carton and as his grandpa worked the lighter, Miles wondered why he didn't smoke the marijuana the doctor prescribed him. From what he'd heard from friends, it wasn't nearly as bad as cigarettes, and it was supposed to make the pain go away.

"Isn't there a chance you could blow us up?"

"I'm the reason you're here at all." His grandpa blew smoke from his chair, skin loose and dry, a dragon guarding a throne, and sipped from his glass. "This is the life, Bobby."

Afraid of getting sick himself, Miles disappeared into his bedroom. He left the door open, his compromise with his grandpa, his mother. Sly wasn't supposed to be alone, but from what Miles could tell, he wasn't.

He opened his laptop with the intention of writing his paper, but when he typed "Apollo 11" into the search bar, the predictive text offered "Apollo 11 hoax." Up until that point, landing on the moon had been matter of fact, its legitimacy completely intact. This crack in the establishment was new to Miles. There were YouTube videos analyzing the discrepancies in lighting and shadows. Yahoo! was littered with questions and arguments, and Reddit featured debates with picture by picture analysis. The flag was waving, some people said, moved by something that wasn't supposed to be there. Some theorists believed that not only was Apollo 11 filmed on a movie set, but that 12 through 14 were staged as well. One link led to another and he fell into a rabbit hole of PDF files and blog posts, but the more he read, the less likely it seemed. The more ambiguous things became, the more he wondered what his grandpa saw in the family room. Miles searched "proof of ghosts" and fell into an additional search that included message boards, apocalyptic warnings, and a video performance by a hologram rapper. He searched and searched and couldn't find an answer for anything. Miles' bedroom floor seemed a few degrees off, the world was no longer definite. Everything could be reexamined.

When his mother returned home to find a full ashtray and an empty glass, save for a few drops of bourbon, she stormed into his bedroom and demanded an explanation. When Miles offered that the moon landing might be fake, that some things weren't as they seemed, she, with her one good arm, scooped his laptop and tossed it to the side. Frays of her blonde hair barely concealed the vein in her forehead and her cheeks blushed as if she'd been cut under the skin, blood pooling beneath a closed surface. The laptop lay on the side, screen still open, an image of a man in a sheet in full screen. Eyes closed, she whispered, "Do you not understand that he's almost gone?"

"He's got company," Miles said. "Shouldn't he be happy?"

Her hand was in her hair, her prosthetic limp at her side. "You savor the last of what you got. You don't down it in one gulp."

"Then let's pour him another." The words fell out of Miles, who was a blend of proud and ashamed. He wanted to take it back but never forget it.

His mother fell silent. Miles waited for her to react, to see what his words meant. Instead, she scooped the laptop and returned to her bedroom. In his closet, Miles found an old black hoodie. It was a hand-me-down, the draw string missing from the hood. He slipped it over his shirt. The sleeves dangled over his hands, the hood almost covered his eyes. It smelled of a wooden box. There was a sharp crash behind the wall as Miles made his way to the kitchen, but he resisted the urge to press his ear to the door. *Black as running mascara?*

In the family room, the television remained on mute. Grandpa Sly was in the kitchen, sifting through the cabinets.

"What do you need?" Miles asked.

"That little brat put them somewhere. Who does she think she is?"

"She probably threw them away."

Grandpa Sly tossed his hands into the air, though they only rose a little past his shoulders. His bald head drooped and he returned to his seat from earlier. He rested his eyes on the newly cloaked Miles, studied him for a bit, and shut them. "She means good," he said.

Miles agreed but he didn't do anything about it just yet. He was too concerned about his paper, and too concerned about his uncle's ghost. "Was the moon-landing staged?"

"Staged?"

"Was it fake?"

"Where's my glass? She took that, too."

Miles grabbed a new glass and dropped two ice cubes in it. He poured more bourbon and set the glass on the table. He pulled a chair out for his grandpa and took the seat to the left of it. "Some people think it was fake."

"Only hopeless believe that shit."

"What about ghosts?"

Grandpa Sly sat in the chair and pinched the loose skin on the top of his head. His teeth were otherwise a complete and yellow set, making the dark gap all the more noticeable. It seemed to project a shadow onto the table, a simultaneous reminder of what had been and what was coming. Miles looked to the bagged tooth on the fridge and was reassured to see nobody had taken it. "Ghosts," his grandpa said. "Ghosts, ghosts, ghosts." He grabbed the glass and traced the creases along the sides that cut into the bottom, creases that contrasted with the unaltered smoothness of his normal glass. "Ghosts are just reminders we didn't set for ourselves." He slid the wrong-glass away.

"Is Bobby a ghost?"

"Bobby," he said and nothing more. He eyed the glass and licked the sides of the teeth that bordered his lost one. "Where's my glass?"

Miles didn't have an answer his grandpa would like but he wanted to know more. "Why did Bobby chop off Mom's arm?"

"Drugs."

"But what did the drugs do?"

"He thought she was going to take him away."

"Away where?"

"The underworld."

Miles hadn't heard this before. He wanted to press his Grandpa further, but not his luck. "Do you remember the first time we landed on the moon?"

Grandpa Sly picked up the glass, sniffed it, but replaced it on the table. "I was in my thirties, I think. We sat around this box with all the lights turned off. Abigail was just in high school, Bobby a few years younger. Greatest moment in advertising. It was so easy to sell when everyone was caught up in wonder. That's the trick, kid. Distract everyone."

Miles thought about something he'd read earlier regarding the government's desire to distract the country from Vietnam. The kitchen fell silent, lending his attention to the hum of the refrigerator. *Black as smoke blowing out an old exhaust?* It roared gently like an engine in the distance, the cicadas sang in beat outside. His eyes fell onto the glass his grandpa refused to drink out of. Miles reached for it, pulled it close, and took a whiff. It reminded him of elementary school, when he'd walk from the bus into the garage, and find his grandpa draped over the hood of his green Impala, gun holstered to his waist. The bourbon had a little less dirt, but gas all the same. Miles took a slow sip. It struggled to go down, gripping at his throat and esophagus until in thrashed in his stomach. After a few breaths, he took another.

Miles' mother joined them in the kitchen, her prosthetic gone now. Miles finished the glass quickly, clenched his teeth and smiled at his mother. The scars, just above where her elbow should've been, crossed like marks he made in Play-Doh as a kid. "What are you two talking about?" she asked and fingered the sleeves of his hoodie.

His grandpa smiled and wheezed out a laugh. "Bobby, go find my glass," he said. He peered over Miles's head, and nodded toward the hallway that joined all of their bedrooms.

"You have another one in your room?" Miles asked.

"No. She took it. Bobby's going to find it."

Miles knew his dead uncle wasn't busting doors down, demanding a glass his mother probably hid, but concern kneaded his gut. His mother looked wounded by his grandpa's words. She put her arm on Sly's shoulder and kissed his lunar head. Miles had only recently begun to understand what it meant to respond to something, but he didn't understand why his mother reacted the way she did sometimes. What made her tick? He hated when people said "itching" when they meant "scratching," or when the girls at his school called hair-ties "pony tails." What did his mother hate, besides his own disobedience? Why wasn't she scared of Bobby?

He kicked his feet as they dangled from his chair. They were heavier than he'd remembered, the kitchen a little wider. "Last year I liked watching cartoons and this year I like reading stuff on the internet," he said. "What will happen next year?"

His mother found a blackhead on his nose and squeezed until a skin larva nestled on her thumb. At the sink she washed her hand by rubbing it against a sponge she kept in the sink. Before she returned to the table, she caught sight of the dead tooth in the bag.

Sly's eyes squeezed tight as he found the long, rectangular light of the kitchen. "In that drawer, the one with the batteries, is a pencil box. Grab it."

Miles found the box and brought it to his grandpa, who opened and pulled out what looked like a cigarette crumpled on both ends. He closed the box, pulled out a lighter, and lit up as he'd done earlier in the day, except when he inhaled, he held it in for a few seconds longer, blowing out of his nose, his shoulders surrendering as he did so. This new smoke was thicker and creamy compared to the wispy, ghost-like smoke of the cigarette. It reeked of something his mother may have cooked on a Thursday, only a few days too late, the ingredients already expired. Sly took another puff and passed the joint to Miles.

Miles looked to his mother, who dangled the bagged tooth in front of her and didn't take the joint away from him. He held it in his fingers, too scared to try anything with it.

"I don't know what to do," Miles said.

"You got to breathe it in, otherwise it doesn't do anything."

"Please, be careful," his mother said.

"I'm tired and I'd like to see this one become a man," Sly said.

Miles put the joint in his mouth, watched the paper shine like the backside of a rocket. He inhaled too much, and coughed the joint onto the floor. He tried to hold it in but he coughed and coughed while his Grandpa Sly laughed and laughed. Miles' mother grabbed his hand and squeezed, and he could feel every bit of helplessness she was sending his way. This was his grandpa's time. They weren't in a position to say no. Miles' chest burned and his eyes grew heavy and he asked, "Why do people like this?"

"Sometimes it's easier to hide," Grandpa Sly said.

"It seems like it'd be easier to die."

"Miles!" his mother said.

Grandpa Sly pushed himself from the table, fumbled with his footing. He took the joint from Miles and pinched it until it crumpled, bits of marijuana sprinkled the floor. "Like the Challenger," he said.

Miles' mother placed her hand on his Grandpa's elbow. His skin draped across her palm. Her stump hung at an angle, an unfeathered wing. Miles realized this must've been what death looked like. He closed his eyes, afraid to look, but the backs of his eyelids were a variegated static. The pulse too menacing to avoid. Miles opened his eyes to an empty kitchen. The bag remained on the table, no dead tooth inside.

Black as a quiet room?

In the family room, Grandpa Sly sat alone in his chair. A purple neck pillow hung below his jaw like the rings of Saturn. His eyes waved like the northern lights. Miles pointed at his grandpa, closed one eye, and twirled his finger as if winding a clock older than himself.

His mother returned with a large blanket and tucked Sly into his chair. Miles reflected on his own bed-making skills, how he struggled to lay a blanket evenly with two arms, and cherished the ease with which his mother fit the blanket snug around his grandpa. The cicadas roared with twice the cavalry. Sly seemingly asleep, Miles' mother turned to him. He raised his hand as if holding a hatchet, sleeve dark and loose, and mimed a chop.

"Explain this," she said, palm outstretched in front of her. The dead tooth rested in the center.

"Preservation," Miles said. "I think." He stopped chopping and grabbed the tooth with his thumb and forefinger. Miles caressed his own vampire teeth with his tongue. In his mouth they felt heavy, but his grandfather's tooth weighed halfway-imagined. "He sees Bobby," Miles said. "He's probably close, right?"

His mother scratched the end of her stump too hard and blood peeked from the center of the doughy crease. She raised it to stop the blood from dripping on the floor and Miles thought of Vesuvius.

He followed her to the sink where she wiped the blood with a damp cloth.

"Are you okay?" he asked.

"Why?"

"I never had a dad, so." Miles didn't want to finish the thought. It wasn't either of their fault. Growing up was learning what was worth saying.

His mother took the tooth from his hand and grabbed the bottle of bourbon he'd poured earlier. "Come with me," she said. From her bedroom, they grabbed Grandpa Sly's glass and walked out onto the back patio.

"Remember that thing we did long time ago?" his mother said. She set the glass down on their patio table. "We put one of your teeth in some Coke, let it rot."

It was a bright memory and one of the first things he'd done with his grandpa. His baby tooth sat in the Coke overnight, and in the morning was a nugget of decay. Miles remembered Grandpa Sly's smile as he pulled the tooth out the glass, his own teeth a yellow horizon. "Be careful what you let in," he'd said. "Plenty of poison in this world."

Miles' mother filled the glass with bourbon, lifted it for a whiff, and returned it to the table. "No sugar in the hard stuff, that's how you know it's for adults," she said and dropped the tooth in the bourbon. "At least that's what he always told me."

The ripple from the drop extended outside the glass and to the edge of Miles' peripheral. His tongue stuck to his teeth like cheap school glue. "What for?" he said.

"Preservation," she said. "I think." She stared at the tooth. Too hard, Miles thought.

Miles pulled the hood off his head and kissed his mother's stump, something he'd never done before. His mother ran her fingers through his hair, scratched the back of his head. "I'm not ready for the silence," she said. "But I'll be okay."

He'd always imagined death to be bigger, something out of orbit. Through the patio window, Miles watched Grandpa Sly sit with his head back and mouth agape. His chest rose and deflated with a shudder. Everything felt quick, like danger in a dream. Behind his grandpa, through the doorway, there was a soft flicker, as if someone had slipped past the hallway light, and Miles understood it was no giant leap.

Goose Island

Chelsea had always been fine in the head. She wasn't prone to anxiety or existential crises, but she was a dedicated med student. She'd wanted to be a doctor since we were in high school when our aunt had throat cancer. Our aunt survived, but it was the chemo that seemed to get to Chelsea. She loved how it made you suffer before you recovered.

She was so dedicated to school work that she'd fall off the grid for weeks at a time. Shut her phone off, hit the books, and still work forty hours a week. I'd only hear from her if she showed up at my door because I lived walking distance from the bar. So when it came time to work with a cadaver and they pulled the sheet back on the third one, she thought she might've recognized it, but couldn't be sure. She snapped a photo and later sent it out in a mass text to friends asking, *anyone know who this is?*

It turned out to be a local hero, Daniel Jeffries, a man that had fostered over a thousand different children in his lifetime. It wasn't long until news traveled to a resident and then an attending, and Chelsea was called into an office where screenshots of the text message were spread out on the desk before her. She showed up at my house clutching a garbage bag of laundry. Clean or dirty it didn't seem to make a difference. Her freckled nose appeared swollen and irritated by excessive wiping. "I've got board games and groceries," I told her.

She pushed past me, up the stairs, into her old bedroom, and didn't emerge for a full day.

It was about four o'clock the next afternoon when she did come out. I was at my drawing table, working on my semi-weekly strip for *The Horseman.* A publisher was interested in a collection, and while the strip was still young, I needed the money. Chelsea crept into the kitchen and asked "What kind of groceries?"

I wasn't sure if she wanted me to tell her or show her. The pencil seemed to lay itself and I grabbed my cutting board and a roll of salami from my fridge. As I pulled the knife from the drawer and prepared to slice, Chelsea made a face, so I replaced the salami and grabbed a box of Frosted Flakes. It seemed less medical. I poured two bowls.

Cereal was our means of bonding, always had been. Television, radio station, or board games, the disagreements on Saturday mornings could be tempered by cereal. It was always Frosted Flakes. While a cartoonist and hesitant to commercialize, I'd always dreamed of designing a cereal box. It was something our father started when we moved south. As a single-parent, he struggled to unite us (I, specifically, was a problem), and only found success by accident. He lazily poured the cereal in a popcorn bowl, dropped three spoons in the thing, and to his surprise, my sister and I bought into it.

Chelsea played with her flakes, and gazed at my drawings that hung on the wall. I'd taken beer brands and drawn them into different animals. "Is that a Yuengling beaver?" she asked.

"Nutria," and I pointed to the swarm of sixty or so nutrias snuggled on the lake shore. They didn't scuffle, or fight, but crept and slept on top of each other. I couldn't remember the last time I'd seen my boat. "I don't know if you've noticed, considering, but it's almost plague-like out there."

"How do you visit Dad?"

In the middle of the lake was a small island that we called Goose Island; for the geese that used to sunbathe there, but also after our father's favorite brewery of the same name. He'd grown up in Chicago, met our mother at the University of Illinois, raised us just outside the city and moved us to central Florida when they divorced. 312 Urban Wheat Ale was his favorite beer. For whatever reason, I hadn't painted that one yet. He died years ago and the pain was no longer raw. We buried him on Goose Island, using two boats to barely row him over. "I don't," I told her.

We finished our cereal and sat together, isolated by our silence. I returned to the strip I was working on, and Chelsea stole a glance. "Getting a bit obsessive, huh?"

"What do you mean?"

"When did your characters become rodents?"

"Don't pretend like you read it." It was an uninteresting piece of something. Comedy? Commentary? Hobbie-try? The general premise centered on two buddies' theological disagreements. It produced a handful of hate mail and death threats, which was a sign of success if you asked certain celebrities, but I was nothing resembling a celebrity. Lately, my two human characters were furry, whiskered and rat-tailed, and I was worried the collection wouldn't sell. The nutria haunted me in a way that had to be deliberate, the fucking swamp rats.

"What are these?" Chelsea asked. She picked up a stack of opened mail, all from the same government agency, a black and incomplete seal stamped in the top right corner.

"Fines. Someone ratted us out," I said and motioned to Goose Island. "I guess there are rules about burying bodies. Sanitation or some shit."

She unfolded one, skimmed it, widened her eyes, and set it back on the table. Her fingers ran through her hair and I could see she was already calculating. How much did she lose by getting kicked out of med school? What would it take it move him? Where would we move him?

"How much do you think the house is worth?" she asked.

"It wouldn't be worth leaving him there," I said. Goose Island was pointless if the house wasn't ours, but that's the way Chelsea worked. She wanted to fix things before weighing them.

Chelsea rose from the table. "Can we play a game? I want to leave, but there isn't anywhere I would go."

"Don't you have an entire class you could call?"

"Very 'Greek Life' over there. When you're in, you're in. When you're out, well..."

"What kind of game?"

"I don't know." She turned and placed her forehead on the wall. "Hide and seek seems a bit melodramatic, right?"

"What about Battleship? One-on-one. Simple."

"No, too random. And a sinking ship is all sorts of morbid."

"Cards?"

"Yes!"

I didn't have any cards, so I slipped on my shoes and left for the Wawa.

Some of the nutria had ventured further than the shore of my backyard into the front, specifically around my mail box. There was nothing there waiting for them, yet there they sat, baring orange teeth as I walked by. They didn't hiss or arch their backs. Actually, they ignored me completely, apathetic of our mutual proximity.

I wondered if I should grab more cereal, or coffee, or tea, but I also didn't know what Chelsea liked. It was always Frosted Flakes and Pepsi. Sometimes, we'd go with Fruity Pebbles and Dr. Pepper, instead, for no reason at all. Now we were adults. We did adult things. I bought a couple of six packs of 312. It wasn't my first choice, but the yellow label shone through the cooler door. Chicago's skyline burned behind the beer's name.

When I returned from Wawa, Chelsea was standing outside, tennis racket in hand.

"Black jack?" I asked.

"We should find the boat."

"We'll need more than this." I grabbed the racket from her hand and tossed it to the side. A couple of nutria scurried away. We walked into the house. "Gin rummy?"

"Only if there's actually gin."

We played a few games, sipping the beer, and Chelsea dominated. In a game composed partially of luck and partially of logic, she was more equipped than me to succeed. She was calculated in a way that led her to medicine and I was distracted in a way that led me to drawing cartoons. Lately, I wondered if the financial strain was worth the freedom to doodle.

"This isn't fun if you never win," she said.

Our father had been pretty competitive with Chelsea, which was probably why she disappeared so quickly after his death. They were always playing and I was always elsewhere. In the same room, but elsewhere. Cleaning our house, I realized how much I'd actually missed over the years. Our carpet was a faded blue, the bathroom mats yellow. The wood floors weren't actually wood and he'd painted "Go Cubbies" into the cushion of his recliner. The more things I discovered, the longer I stayed, and my pencil produced more strips. There was still plenty of house to uncover and I had infinite time to make up for.

There had been a few times in our childhood in which I could beat Chelsea in games of strategy. She may have been better at counting cards, but I was better at reading her poker face. Her freckles would grow bold as her cheeks flushed red. The wrinkle between her eyebrows rolled when she was flustered. When we played Risk, I'd always win the war, if only because I understood the sacrifice each piece was making. The dice were inconsequential in a game of imaginary life and death.

But that had been long ago, before Chelsea started med school, before our aunt's rounds of chemo.

We filled our glasses again, and Chelsea looked outside often. Goose Island was wild; the grass several feet long, its one tree flaccid and without fight. It was usual for our father's grave to be out of sight, but I could sense her fear that it'd disappeared. A fear that it'd been neglected for too long. She didn't say anything, though.

The unspoken truth was that it probably had disappeared, dangling that close to sea level. His coffin more than likely sank through the bottom of the island and to the bottom of the lake. When we dug, we only made it about three and half feet deep before water seeped into the grave. Despite the callouses on our hands, the sharp ache in our arms from digging and dumping, the hole insisted on filling itself. I remember pondering fate, then suggesting the blankets on the boat we'd used as seat cushions, hoping they would soak the water up. Though it provided no confirmation, visitation was our only solace.

"We can't smack them all with a tennis racket," I said.

"Maybe we can light a fire? Scare them with torches?" She was already searching through my drawers, pulling out a lighter.

"We'd be better off soaking them in lighter fluid."

"Do you have any?"

"How about we decide on dinner first?"

With little discussion, I ordered a pizza and disappeared to my bedroom to change my clothing. The end of baseball season was approaching and the Cubs were set to clinch a wild-card spot. Though our father didn't teach us faith, he taught us superstition. He'd left me his Ernie Banks jersey and if I didn't wear it all nine innings, I would struggle with sleep for a week, calculating playoff odds in my dreams. The Cubbies were my responsibility now.

The summer before I graduated high school, our father planned a two-week trip to Chicago. The itinerary included a visit to our grandparents' graves, a Cubs-White Sox double-header, several pictures by the Bean, and dinner with our mother. His sickness was his motivation, but he hadn't disclosed that to us. The dinner with our mother was non-negotiable and eighteen, self-righteous, and stupid, I refused to go. He didn't argue with me, but instead put pizza money in an envelope and left it in the fruit bowl. Infuriated by the ease with which they abandoned me, I didn't bother watching the game on television. He passed in the bottom of the sixth of game two, the Cubbies down by one. Chelsea drove him home in a rental and we never talked about our mother.

As I buttoned my jersey, my blue cap ragged and cocked a little to the left, a lawnmower started up outside. A startling roar, considering it was almost eight now, and my neighbors lived a couple hundred feet away on each side. It wasn't until I was flipping through my channels that I realized the sound was coming from my own backyard.

Outside, Chelsea stood with her hands on the mower, seeming to deliberate where to start. The nutria covered the majority of my yard, some had retreated closer to the water at the rumble of the mower, and I put my hand on her shoulder. "We don't have to do this. We'll find a way."

She stared at Goose Island, squeezing the handle. "It's different when not seeing people is my choice. You don't miss them as much when there's the option not to." She started forward, pushing towards the river, and succeeded in scaring away the nutria. They squirmed and shuffled in an animated panic.

"You have me. I'm still a choice," and I wasn't sure if I said it or simply thought it because the only sound I heard was Chelsea's roar to the backdrop of the motor. She pushed in no particular direction, leaving an awful pattern of high grass in my lawn.

The sun was setting behind us, behind the house, and the far end of the lake had already grown navy and active. Nutria entered the lake in waves, submerging themselves completely save for their snouts. They left ripples akin to those of toy boats. When it seemed all had entered the water, I noticed that the few left on the shore hadn't budged because they were dead, squashed or suffocated by the other nutria around them.

My boat was visible now, and I was happy that I'd left it unturned, otherwise it would have become a nutria coffin. A mass rodent grave. Chelsea cut the motor and I flipped the boat over. It was a small thing, about eight feet long, with one oar and built for fishing. It was made of plywood, I think, painted blue with "Chelsea" engraved across the side in red. There was a second boat marked "Logan" after me, but it cracked under the weight of our father's coffin and sank when I tried to row it back.

I pushed it closer to the shoreline and asked Chelsea if she wanted to go tonight.

She didn't answer and I turned to find her standing over one of the nutria I'd thought to be dead. It lay on its side, tail flat on the grass, its webbed toes curled in a stubborn grasp for life. Every few seconds or so, its side would rise with breath.

"It isn't dead, yet," Chelsea said. She pushed the mower to the side and squatted closer to the nutria. It didn't budge. "What do we do?"

"You're the doctor," I said.

Chelsea disappeared inside and I held the boat in place so it wouldn't drift away. She returned with a towel, laid it next to the nutria, and flipping the towel over the nutria, wrapped it like a sleeping child. She cradled it in her arms and approached the boat. I wanted to ask what she was doing, but I didn't think she would've told me, had she known or not. She stepped in the boat, sat on one end and balanced the towel on her lap. I told her to wait and ran inside, into my kitchen, where I grabbed one of the six-packs from the fridge and returned outside. I pushed the rest of the boat into the water and hopped into the other end.

"What's with the beer?"

"What's with the swamp rat?"

We drifted towards Goose Island, only using the oar to keep us on track. The sun was gone and the wild life awake. The few ducks left quacked out of sight and insects reverberated in the trees. Around us, nutria swam absently and steady, unafraid of our creeping vessel, which reeked of wet dog. Chelsea hugged the towel close. She closed her eyes. The water rocked the three of us.

"How are you going to save it?" I asked her, assuming most human medicine could be applied to animals. I pictured Chelsea laying the river rat on my ironing board, wearing my yellow dishwashing gloves, and blue bandana over her mouth. She'd take the knife I almost used earlier and make a long but shallow incision. "To relieve the pressure," she'd say. "So it can properly heal," or some shit like that. Then I'd draw it and hang it in her old bedroom.

"It never had a chance," she said. The boat reached Goose Island. Chelsea's end slid on to the shore.

"Then what are you doing?"

"I didn't want it to die alone."

The sentiment hurt me. I hadn't considered it myself.

We hopped out of the boat and pulled it completely on shore. The island was incredibly small, maybe a hundred feet across. In the moonlight and through the high grass we found our father's headstone. Chelsea carried the nutria with her as we approached his grave. A few nutria scampered to the other side of the island.

I set the six pack next to his head stone where a dozen of other packs sat uninterrupted. A few of the bottles were empty, caps lost in the wild, from the days I had cartoonists' block. I couldn't remember the last time I'd been there so I opened a bottle on the end of the boat and poured some of the beer on the grave. Chelsea laughed as the soil fizzed below.

She held the nutria closer to her chest, her eyebrow wrinkle rolled. "I made a mistake even you couldn't fix," she said. "I'm glad you missed it."

From Goose Island my lawn looked like an aftermath. Nutria returned and squirmed in groups. My television flashed through a window on the far side and I imagined the Cubs were winning, if only because we needed them to. There was a cartoon somewhere in all of this, I thought, but wouldn't find it until later.

I turned back to the grave and Chelsea was on her knees. Nutria in one arm, she pulled earth away with the other. The roots popped as she ripped them from underneath. She clawed and tossed but made little progress.

"What are you doing?"

"If this is going to be a thing, then I have to know," she said.

"It's not like we'll be able to carry him. We barely got him over here."

But she kept digging. I offered to take the nutria from her, but she shook her head, and I found myself on my knees, clawing with both hands. The soil was moist in a lively way, and I expected worms and beetles to crawl from the dirt in my palms. Small waves splashed onto the shore of Goose Island. With each scoop, a panic reverberated within me. Subtle, then exponentially worse. An unintelligible desperation struck and I dug like a dying ground hog.

We were about a foot deep and Chelsea stopped. "It's dead now." She stood up, nutria still cradled in her arms, and walked softly to the boat. I dumped the dirt from my hands and joined her.

"Did it help?" I asked, my breath short, still exhausted from the stupid panic.

"It did this thing, where it reached for my shirt." Chelsea grasped at the air in front of her.

"So that's it?" I asked, and Chelsea took a seat inside the boat. I lingered by the grave, unnerved by the piles of dirt. I wanted to replace them, pat it all down and make it neat again.

"You're fine, Logan," she said, and beckoned me with her free hand. "Leave it."

And I did. I pushed the boat back into the lake, hopped in and set us adrift once again. On opposite sides now, the moon illuminated Chelsea's dry eyes. We were halfway to my yard when she asked me to wait a minute.

"I've got to let it go," she said.

We rocked in place and water splashed inside. The flash of my television was brighter, the dank smell of the lake a little stronger. Chelsea leaned over the edge and rolled the dead nutria in the water. It splashed, and rolled and bobbed in the rippling lake.

As the body drifted away from us, the current of the lake shifted. Having swum with no structure or pattern before, many of the nutria now swam in a single direction, towards us as a singular unit. No particular formation, but together they approached the dead nutria floating by our boat, and the two at the head of the pack nudged the body forward with their snouts. Whiskers tickling the surface, they swam on, others close behind. They pushed, carrying the body around Goose Island and out of sight.

We drifted back to my yard to find the other dead nutria gone as well, seemingly removed by the others, and as we stepped out of the boat, the lake was empty and peaceful in a way I hadn't known before.

"So that's what it's like," Chelsea said.

Unsolicited Independence

The dust around my television is out of control. It's layered so much that it floats like the mist of the retention pond. My brother doesn't say anything about it. He's telling me about some joke, or jokes, he's been working on.

"It's like a self-help seminar, except a stand up special, but it's all real advice." His eyes are wide, scared, and he's smiling at me.

"Sounds like you'd need more than ten minutes."

"Well, this isn't for now. This is for when I make it."

"Nick."

"What?"

"What happened, man?"

His hands drop and he's no longer looking at me. He shrugs his shoulders and shakes his head.

"Your message came out of nowhere," I say. Underneath my desk is a wrapped present. Pacifiers and a Jaguars baby blanket.

"I woke up to her kicking me in the head. Screaming at me, telling me to stop talking shit. That other people didn't need to know our business."

"What business?"

"Fuck, man. Anything, I guess." He's squeezing his biceps. Though younger, he's much bigger than me. "So anyway, I don't freak out, you'd be proud. I tell her she needs to go to her mom's."

I squeeze his head with my hand. It's an old thing I do, even if my hands are too small now. "Was there an accident? Did she fall?"

"She comes over the next day, tells me she spent the night in the emergency room. That she lost the baby. Something about the commotion, I don't know. Then she packed her shit."

We pour the bourbon I was saving for another twenty weeks or so. "Have you spoken since?"

"Not to her. There's this waitress at the Ale House."

He isn't joking. Nick hasn't been alone since he was fifteen. He was married at twenty-one, divorced at twenty-three, father-to-be six months after that and now talking to a waitress. She is probably a nice girl, too, but will turn sour when Nick's love turns out to only be a deep and scathing affection. He's standing by the television now, drawing a dick in the dust. His glass is empty.

We scheduled this night to exchange gifts and I'm desperate to think of something else. I don't think he's noticed the Toy Story wrapping paper. Woody's large eyes won't leave me alone. They follow me when I look away. I should've grabbed the Buzz Lightyear paper. That was Nick's choice as a kid. Woody was my character.

"It all seems fast, doesn't it?" I say.

He passes me his glass. I fill it. I fill mine.

"How've you done it? Manage it. Make sense of it?" he asks. He's holding his glasses, modern black frame, twirling them with his eyes closed. "I mean, Jared straight up left you." He catches himself. Nick knows he's hurt me but doesn't reach out.

The condos across the lake are bright and my neighbors are completely naked save for a couple of Santa hats. Not just one unit, but six of the nine units are bright and full of naked people. I'm sure each of them thinks they're the only one. What are coincidences anyway?

My friend Cristina bought her husband an acre on the moon for Christmas. I tell this to Nick.

"There's someone out there that sells moon to people? What for?"

"For their children. Or the grandchildren. Whatever comes first."

Nick buckles over. His hands squeeze the cushions beneath him. His head is almost resting on the coffee table.

I rub the massive back of my little brother and think about the time a fourth grader threw a stick at him, a third grader and small. It slashed him across his face. Nick erupted with tears. I, a fifth grader, punched the fourth grader in the face. His blood was hot on my knuckles.

There isn't anyone I can punch for Nick now. Upright, he makes a face, the same as when the stick struck him, with a kind of permanence this time. I put my hand on his head again, squeeze the loose skin beneath his hair.

"I love you," I say, with that blunt sort of urgency you use when you really need someone to hear it.

He folds into me, and though I can't fit my arms around him, I know he loves me too. There's an illness in him, a flu of the heart that will get better but never go away. I don't know the remedy for that, I'm still figuring it out myself.

SUPRA-TERRESTRIAL

Scoop Carry Dump Repeat

Kevin stands in the comic book section of The Book barn because he hasn't quite grasped accountability. He's supposed to be at the Publix, grabbing a pregnancy test, but he stares at the copy of *Homicidal Psycho Jungle Cat*. He reaches for it then drops his hand at his side.

"Can I help you find something?" an employee says to him. Purple hair frames a crooked face. She keeps her distance and Kevin thinks he scares her.

"I'm not ready."

"You can't drink here," and she is gone.

Kevin finishes the beer in his hand and slides the bottle into a flaccid end of the book shelf. He slides out of The Book Barn, hops on his bike and rides to the Publix. He grabs the cheapest brand of tests and pedals home to Susan.

Twenty-one years ago, on his eighth birthday, the first since his mother had left, his father gave him a single gift. Kevin traced his fingers along the edges, noticed how it wagged in his hands. He pressed a soft nail into the Sunday Funnies and peeled the paper back to reveal a large book. On the cover was an image of a boy and a tiger in a tree, donning paper sailor hats, and a water balloon they'd just hurled towards an unsuspecting little girl.

"Inde-indip?" he said.

"*The Indispensable Calvin and Hobbes,*" his father said. He sat behind him, pulled Kevin into his lap, his leather jacket engulfing the two of them. "It's a comic book."

"Like Batman."

His father opened the cover and flipped through the first couple of pages. "Not quite."

More books followed, sprinkled throughout the timeline of his life. The third quarter of fourth grade, Kevin earned straight A's for the first time, and rather than the complete set of Topps football cards he'd hoped for, his father gave him *Something Under the Bed is Drooling*. When he hit his first homerun in little league, he came home to *Weirdos from Another Planet*, and when he was sixteen, after spending four hours of his Saturday taking the SATs, his father surprised him with *The Calvin and Hobbes Tenth Anniversary Book*.

The routine continued, culminating at the distribution of his father's estate a couple of weeks ago. It'd only been the two of them. They were a team. So, yes, he got the house. The 220,000 dollars so. The '89 Oldsmobile. Kevin nodded until the attorney dropped a cardboard box taped end to end. He was handed a box cutter and sliced it open. Inside, he found what looked every Calvin and Hobbes book he'd yet to receive from his father.

There was *Yukon Ho*! and *The Calvin and Hobbes Lazy Sunday Book* and there was *Calvin and Hobbes*, the first collection, but there was no copy of *Homicidal Psycho Jungle Cat*. Kevin asked if there was anything else.

"Just this box."

"No more books?"

And the attorney reaffirmed there were no more books, only those in the box.

Published on his seventh birthday, *Homicidal Psycho Jungle Cat* was the only book he ever asked for, and was now the only book he didn't have.

"If you want it, go get it. Nobody's stopping you," his father would say, his voice an even-laid gravel.

Except Kevin preferred the books be a gift from his father, a bridge between the two of them, an inheritance that wouldn't dissipate. He continued to ask his father for *Jungle Cat* and his father continued to tell him, "Nobody's stopping you."

"You know what I've noticed, Hobbes? Things don't you bug you if you don't think about them."

Susan sits in bed, glasses on her nose, dark hair balanced in a wet bun. Something flashes from the television. It's the third time this week Kevin's come home drunk. He drops the tests on the bed and jumps in the shower before she says anything about the smell, his sagging eyes.

The sound of Susan peeing echoes off the tiled walls of the shower. Kevin sits lotus while the water beats his face.

"Moe left another note," she says through the curtain.

"What is that? Six?"

"We should say something."

Kevin cuts the water. Susan now sits in bed with two tests in front of her. He settles in close to her and her bun drips on his shoulder.

"He'll take the hint eventually." Their history with Moe has grown fairly contentious. Whether it's a stray beer can or the ten inches of Oldsmobile bumper that extends into Moe's "territory" (he seems to believe he is Riverside royalty), he hasn't failed to share the transgression in zig-zagged handwriting. Kevin occasionally catches him in the window, his shifty eyes peering from behind shaggy hair, studying the frayed and twisted ends of the hedges. At night, Moe's clumpy-haired porch cat mews and scratches until dawn, but god forbid his neighbor's lawn get a little wild.

"At some point, you have to do something," Susan says and hands Kevin a test. They each hold them eye-level.

His reads a single vertical line. Negative.

They trade. The other test is double lines. Positive.

Kevin collects the tests and walks into the kitchen, looks for another beer. He sets the tests atop the fridge and cracks something crafty and blueberry, all that's left. The box of Calvin and Hobbes books rests on the kitchen table.

The beer tastes like soggy cereal. By the time he finishes, it's officially night and Kevin deflates with the speed at which a day passes. There's no time for anything, just white space between scenes. A car horn sings. A cat screeches at an inconvenience.

When he returns, Susan is finishing a phone call and he's reminded he fell in love with her phone voice. Soft, formal, a little fabricated in her laughs. Susan's smile reveals a little too much gum. She's losing patience with him, he's losing patience with the world. Why aren't things fixed, yet? Susan ends the call. "Don't be out too late tomorrow, we're going to see my parents," she says. She clicks her lamp off and turns to sleep. Kevin dreams of expanding bellies, awakens when they burst.

The next day, school ends, his tenth graders storm out, and Kevin rides his bike to the gas station and scoops a road brew. He cruises to The Book barn and floats down the comic book aisle, once again stares at their only copy of *Homicidal Psycho Jungle Cat.*

A thin black book, the average browser will pass by without a glance. Kevin reaches for it, hesitates, and pulls the collection from the shelf. On the cover, Calvin appears to be sleep-walking, unaware of his stuffed-tiger Hobbes soaring above him mid-pounce. Kevin shakes the book and replaces it.

He imagines his father floating from an empty space in the shelf, pulling *Jungle Cat,* and eating it with his ghost mouth (ghosts eat anything, right?). If Susan is pregnant, maybe this would be the special occasion his father had been waiting for.

If Susan is pregnant, he's been too distracted to prepare himself. Bits of life have been falling through the cracks, chasing his father into whatever follows, the white space.

He again grabs the book, finishes his beer while the purple-haired girl rings him up, and walks out to his bike.

Book in one hand, the handle bars in another, Kevin can't respond to his buzzing phone. He hops over tree roots and swerves around street cats. He ducks underneath low-hanging limbs and spits at stop signs as he wisps by. At his home, he ditches his bike in the front lawn, where it disappears beneath wild and high-reaching grass that needed to be cut three months ago, and jumps the steps to his porch. Kevin tries the door but finds it locked. He pats his pockets, realizes he doesn't have his keys, and Susan's bike isn't locked to their mailbox. He calls her but the phone goes to voicemail. He tries again.

Taped to the door is a new note from Moe: *Please for the sake of our kingdom, cut your lawn.*

Kevin sits, back to the door, head against the frame. He could fall asleep there, a womb kind of drunk.

"So from now on, I simply won't think about anything I don't like, and I'll be happy all the time!"

He awakens on his porch, *Homicidal Psycho Jungle Cat* in his lap. He wishes he hadn't had so much to drink. He hopes that Susan isn't pregnant, if only because this isn't how he wants to remember it. He's only drinking because otherwise he'll pace, antagonized by dead air, that white space.

Kevin ponders the curvature of time, the karma of staying still. His in-laws don't live too far, so he carries the book and returns to his bike. They'll avoid eye-contact with him, but that's okay. At least he'll have arrived. He hops over tree roots and approaches a street cat basking in the dark that he thinks will get out of the way, so he doesn't swerve, and without breaking, the front wheel collides with the feline. Kevin lurches forward and falls onto the sidewalk below.

Scraped elbows and swelling shoulder, he uses one hand to toss his bike to the side and watches the street cat, which he now recognizes as Moe's, wobble side-to-side back toward its home. It seems alright except that its head is cocked to the left, gentle in its posture. Kevin's eyes follow it until it trips over a curb, mewing into the homes around them. The chain on his bike lies limp, popped off the gear and he doesn't see the copy of *Homicidal Psycho Jungle Cat* anywhere. He stumbles, searching the grass, scanning and scanning but no luck. In the street, he drops to the asphalt and peers underneath cars parked along the curb. Nothing under the Volvo, the Mazda, or the Camry. A green truck starts up behind him, pulls out from behind the Volvo and drives away. In the abandoned parking space Kevin finds nothing, an oil stain. He considers the travelling truck bed.

He leaves his bike and follows the truck on foot. The string of stop-signs in the neighborhood allow him to maintain a semblance of pace until the truck hooks a left and drives toward the strip. Kevin reaches the intersection and catches the taillights pulling into a parking spot outside the dive bar. He sprints across the five-way intersection, absorbing honks and shouts as he runs, and leaps his way to the parked truck. He peeks inside the bed and spots his copy of *Homicidal Psycho Jungle Cat.*

It isn't within reach, and he's unsure which shop the driver disappeared to. Kevin places one foot on the top of the back tire and pulls himself into the bed. It bounces with his added weight and the driver's door opens up.

"What's up?" says a large man in a black polo. He approaches Kevin and the truck bed.

"My book," Kevin says and scoops it up, wags it in the man's face.

The man swipes *Jungle Cat* from him and studies it. After a moment, he tosses it into the middle of the street. "Get out of my truck," he says and walks into the nearby cinema.

Kevin bounces out the truck. A trio of bikers roar over the book.

He fans away lingering exhaust, retrieves *Jungle Cat* from the street and for a moment, considers returning to the bar, grabbing another drink. A homeless gentleman pets a turtle on a stool outside the dog hotel. A few honks and Kevin finds himself wandering through the smoke and dim lighting to a rocky stool. He orders a beer and inspects the large, lumpy crease across the cover of the book. The pages seem okay but he doesn't look inside. Not yet. He isn't sure any of this is permanent, but rather some looney purgatory that may return to normal at any moment. This is better anyway, he'd rather not be a mess in front of Susan's parents. The bartender brings him his drink and waves his cash away.

"It's on her," she says and points across the bar where underneath a purple neon light sits his small, sweatered mother. She's a worn edition of his memory, but her eyes, the 80s curls. It's her.

There's an impulse to thrash about, but he's an adult and prefers to do something a little more lasting. He wants to splash the drink on her forehead and watch it wash away her make-up. He wants the people of the bar to applaud his stand. He wants a reckoning. Kevin grabs the glass, and thinks about taking the beer into his mouth, spitting it in her face. He thinks about this and other punishments, and his mother takes a seat next to him.

"I'm sorry about your dad," she says. "I'm sorry about me, too."

He places his hands on the bar, ready to push himself back, but he doesn't. His mother's eyes bore in the side of his head and anchor him in place.

"All anyone would tell me was that he collapsed."

"Heart attack," Kevin hears himself say and he can't stop. "He was mowing the lawn, like every Sunday, waiting for the game to come on." He doesn't know why he's telling her anything.

"Two more beers," his mother says.

The last time he saw his mother was at the wake, sipping from a flask right outside the front door, her hair a back drop to space ship eyes.

The time before that was right before the start of the third grade. Undressed, hair stuck, he walked into his parents' bedroom where he found his father getting dressed. "Where's Mom?" Kevin said.

"You know your mother," his father said. He struggled with tucking his tie underneath the back of his collar, like his mother would sometimes struggle with her back zipper. "She comes, and she goes."

Kevin thought about this, the familiarity of it. "Can we have Pop-Tarts for breakfast?"

"Absolutely. Today is your day."

He didn't think much about his mother until the end of the school year, when during a Mother's Day celebration, a substitute teacher played stand-in for the vacant spot at his side. She was blonde, freckle-armed and bathed in a sharp perfume. After that, he stopped waiting for his mother's arrival and constructed her around half the dichotomy. She goes, forgetting there was ever another half at all.

"Don't you think that's a pretty silly and irresponsible way to live?"

"Calvin and Hobbes," his mother says. "I remember sending you one of these a long time ago."

Kevin hugs the copy of *Homicidal Psycho Jungle Cat* close to him and shuts his eyes. He feels ridiculous. High school algebra teacher with the dead dad and the comic strip obsession. He considers the truth of her words, whether there's any reason to trust them, and remembers that if Susan is pregnant, it would be this woman's grandchild. The notion goes boom within.

"I'm getting married at the end of the year," Kevin says. He finishes the beer, turns the glass over. He takes his mother's face in his hands. "It worked out for me," he says.

Her face contorts in his hands and he lets her go.

"This isn't real," he says. He squeezes the book. "Not when he can't be here." Kevin feels off-course, a little heavy on one side.

His mother doesn't say anything. Mascara runs into the cracks of her skin and thoughtlessly, Kevin wipes it with a cocktail napkin. The makeup leaves a symmetrical splotch on the paper, something like an ink-blot, and he crumples it in his fist. His mother places her hand on his elbow. It's cold from holding her drink, almost life-less, and Kevin pulls his arm away. He tosses the cocktail napkin in her lap. "This is fine," he says and leaves the bar.

He cuts across the intersection and veers onto his street without looking. His bike lies where he left it so he grabs it and pushes it home. There's a sharp mewing in the distance. Cars no longer line the street. The popped chain drags like the feet a stubborn child. Kevin pushes his bike into his front lawn where it disappears into the grass, which has to have grown in the past hour. He doesn't see Susan's bike and tries the front door again, just in case, but no luck.

The note from Moe looms larger than before. The jagged handwriting curves and cuts like the mascara on his mother's face. The mewing is louder and comes in quick succession. Kevin tears the note from the door. He hops down his porch and crosses the tangled mess into Moe's trimmed lawn. Up the steps, swelling within, he drops the crumpled note in the bushes, proud of his litter, and bangs on the front door.

After a moment, no response.

He rings the doorbell. "Open up, you sonofabitch." Hands cupped around his eyes, he peers into the windows. More mewing comes from nowhere until Moe's long-haired porch cat waddles from around the corner. Its head still cocks to the left, its tail wide-right to counter the imbalance. It hops onto the railing of the porch, stumbles, but catches itself. It does something high pitched at Kevin. "Go on," he says. "Get him out here."

The cat falls silent, eyes locked onto him. It licks its nose. Kevin waits for it to meow again, to cry as it always does. It feigns like it may, but instead stretches its mouth wide and yawns.

"Come on, I know that neck's got to hurt." Kevin reaches for the cat and scratches it behind the ear. It sinks its teeth into the meaty pad beneath his thumb and retreats, its equilibrium operating at bare minimum. His hand stings, his head thumps. Kevin reaches for the cat again, quickly, and it jumps for the angled roof. Its forepaws land, it claws for safety, and falls into the yard below. It lands on its side, turning its neck a bit more, and lies limp in a pool of streetlight.

Kevin hops to the cat. He nudges it with the inside of his shoe and flips it as he would a skateboard. Its open eyes have a wild tint to them, a blend of the gray night and the orange hue of the lights around. There's a hushed zipping behind him. He turns to spot Susan gliding to their house where she locks her bike to the mailbox.

She's wearing her blue dress, the one she wears with a smile, and crosses their knotted grass. She briefly notes Kevin's abandoned bicycle and disappears behind the front door. Kevin looks back to the cat, assures himself it is dead, and bolts over the hedges.

Susan opens the door, brow low and disappointed, and he pushes past her to the kitchen. Pours himself a drink.

"Mom and Dad were sad you couldn't make it," she says. She hovers near him, but Kevin doesn't know what to say. He gives her to the book to hold.

She looks as though she could cry.

"His cat is dead. It leapt and fell and now it's dead," he says.

Susan leans between the opening into the kitchen. "Moe's cat?"

Kevin nods and downs his drink. "I'm sorry I didn't show."

Susan shrugs and the passivity is unfamiliar to him. Is this surrender? "If we leave it, he'll think it died naturally," she says.

"I have to get rid of it. He shouldn't have to see." Kevin grabs a backpack from the closet and dumps remnants from his childhood onto the floor below. He carries it outside, through the grasping grass, and into Moe's yard.

The cat's eyes are still open and wild, its teeth half-bared. Street lights cast shadows of tree limbs that seem to reach for the cat, coercing it to join them. Kevin peeks over his shoulder to see Susan watching. Her hand rests on her stomach, a maternal magnetism. He grabs the cat by the back of the neck, the skin not quite stiff yet, and forces it head-first into his back pack. He pulls the zipper and after a couple of tugs, Kevin manages to zip up most of the cat, save for a half-limp tail that sticks out to the right.

Back in his house, Susan offers to take it for him. "I've got it," she says, but he holds onto the back pack.

Kevin imagines the length of Moe's next note, an accusatory flier etched across their entire door. He looks through the front window. His father's red Oldsmobile shines garnet in the night.

Susan flips the pages of *Homicidal Psycho Jungle Cat* against her fingers. She looks at the back pack. "I read the baby is the size of a poppy seed right now. Sesame seed next week."

Kevin takes the book and tucks it underneath his arm once again. He grabs the keys from the hook in the wall, throws the cat-full pack over his shoulder. That's smaller than her pupils, he thinks.

Susan squeezes his hands, hesitant to let him go, but he pulls them away and places them on her hips. He kisses her cheek and says, "Thank you," before slipping out the front door into the Oldsmobile.

"What a pretty afternoon."

He pulls the car into his father's driveway, parks, and sits still for a moment. The garage in front of him, the leather of his father's wheel in his palms, it blankets him with a permanence. He avoids looking at the tailed-bag to his right, and grabs the copy of *Homicidal Psycho Jungle Cat.* He opens to a strip on page fifteen in which Cavin answers a phone call from someone trying to reach his mother. He offers to give her a message so long as the other caller writes it down, drives over, and pays fifteen bucks. The strip ends with Calvin saying, "He must not have wanted to talk to Mom very bad." Kevin chuckles, just once at first, and when he rereads he laughs more, this time full and hearty. Soon his rib cage aches and his laughter remains stuck in his throat. He wipes his eyes dry, closes the book, and sets it down before it can do anymore damage.

He opens his father's garage door. On the wall hang various garden tools: rakes, hoes, hedge trimmers, and other sticks with ends he'd seen his father use over the years. He pulls the shovel with a pointed tip from the wall and drags it to the yard. He scans the lawn, falls into the past. Grass stains, lizard catching, cat feeding, ball throwing, hose spraying. His father didn't maintain the yard for neighborly appeasement or his own neurosis. It was always about the memory. Kevin knows this, but he hates it anyway.

He presses the tip into the ground, pushes his foot on the top of the head, and drives it down. Roots resist at first, but give away and

Kevin lifts the ground up, over, and out of the way. He repeats. He digs and digs, and avoids going too deep. This is a punishment, not a grave. Few neighbors stroll by, but they know the story. They saw him egg the house. They found his father's face in the dirt. They pass and don't ask questions, avoiding the son caught between the stages of grief. They all pass except his mother, who fades in from white space.

"Need any help?" she says.

Kevin shakes his head.

But she steps closer, watching Kevin dig.

"Jesus. You don't exist to us."

"I wanted to see the house."

He continues digging. If he keeps digging, she'll figure it out and leave. He spears the shovel back into the dirt and finds he can only go so deep. Sweat drips from his nose, his armpits, the shore of his hairline.

"Let me be here," she says.

Kevin tosses the shovel to the side. "You want to help? Here," he says. He tosses the keys at her feet. "Grab that back pack and bring it to me."

She opens the car and momentarily disappears, a ghost in a graveyard.

Out of the car, bag in hand, his mother studies the long-haired tail that sticks out sideways. She taps the end with a finger and carries it to Kevin. He imagines the bag wiggling in her arms, the cat alive and shaking itself free. Maybe it would jump at her, mistake her for the one on the zipping bicycle. Instead, it dangles motionless on her shoulder. It seems heavier as she approaches. Kevin takes the bag, unzips it, and dumps the cat into the grave. Together they study it, clumpy and unaware, its face frozen in shock. As he stands there, Kevin imagines the roots reaching out, wrapping the body in a welcoming embrace. He picks the shovel up and buttresses himself for a moment.

"Is that real?" his mother says.

"Yes."

"Are you going bury it, then?"

"I need a minute."

His mother pulls the shovel from him. She walks to the other side where Kevin piled the dirt, and shovels it back into the hole. Scoop, carry, dump, repeat. The hole fills. Kevin watches her sweat and pant while she buries a mistake. Soon the cat will disappear, the grass will repair itself, and the rest of the world will move on. Dirt covers the wild eyes.

Kevin grabs the copy of *Homicidal Psycho Jungle Cat* from the car. He steps to the hole and holds the book over it, ready to drop. He studies the cover, the bits of Moe's cat still visible beneath the dirt, his mother's face; looking for instruction. Shadows fill the cracks below her eyes, and Kevin doesn't know what to do.

"I remember reading those in the paper, when you were in your high chair."

He drops it in the hole. When she reaches for it, he says, "Leave it."

And she does. Kevin takes the shovel from her, continuing the burial until the cat and Calvin and Hobbes are out of sight. When the hole is filled, he returns the shovel to the garage wall. He steps into his father's home, into the kitchen and leaves the door open behind him. In the morning, he'll have to replace the grass and mow his own. He'll have to return to normal. He'll go to The Book Barn and scoop a book of baby names. He grabs the bourbon his father kept on the top of the fridge and pours two glasses. He drinks his, refills, and waits.

Cages

Sometimes I miss the blisters that form from the bat sliding in my hands, so I go to Adventure Zone where I get a hundred-forty pitches for ten bucks. I only do this occasionally, but when I do it's because the itch is almost unbearable. I'm the most uncomfortable when my hands are smooth and my obliques sans ache.

I used to bring a six pack, pound a beer between tokens, but I'm married now and I have to get home safely. Instead, I buy three extra tokens (sixty more pitches), so I can feel the bruising in each turn of my torso a few days longer. Two hundred pitches, a good sweat, and I can feel my body climb the three flights to my condo.

The first token hurts less than you'd expect. My eyes are fresh because the sweat hasn't pooled and the attendants haven't walked by to tell me to put a helmet on. I have enough energy to really turn on the inside pitches. The second token is tough because I switch sides and bat left handed even though I'm left-eye dominant, and I'm a little late the first few swings which really rattles my inner palm. My left knee isn't as accustomed to the twisting movement, and soreness comes quick. I prefer to bat left-handed.

Iguanas between three and four feet in length roam Adventure Zone for no advertised reason. They whip their tails and pay no mind to the teenagers tongue-jousting in the gazebos. They usually squirm themselves into the caged dome around the third and fourth tokens, and fortunately, I never hit them. In fact, this is usually when I whiff thirty of the next forty pitches. A good cage sesh has peaks and valleys, like a mixtape you make for yourself as you drive into a hurricane. Now that I don't bring the beers, I seem to miss more.

It's always in the middle of the sixth token that the attendants ask me to put a helmet on. I know because I'm batting left-handed, and they startle me, I whiff, and the ball recoils off the padding behind me into the back of my head. I wear the helmet for the sixth token, which turns out to be a good thing because the visor over my eyes relaxes me and after a hundred or so pitches my body fights continued swings. This is my only work out, and it comes every three to nineteen weeks.

Around the seventh token the first blister opens up. The sweat pools with the grime of the bat handle and the sting reminds me to get the bat off my shoulder, to hit the ball with a sense of urgency. Sometimes I get lazy like that, just cutting through pitches, timing them but not really swinging at them. When the skin on my palm folds back, I see the pitches a little bigger. They swell into yellow tumors and the bat pops them across the cage.

There's always some kind of older man with chicken legs and a golf cap taking cuts in the slow-pitch softball cage at the end. These dudes irk me in a way that turns my neck hot. Their arrival times vary, but this night they show up during the eighth token and I swear the iguanas snicker like cicadas in the trees. When these dudes show up I let one of the balls go back untouched so they know I'm in the fastest baseball cage and rip a few good ones off the sweet spot. The slow-pitch softball cage? How do they live?

Occasionally the eight-year-old with the weak hands will cry because he hit one with the inside of the bat and I have to pause until his parents finally take him home. Other times the local high school softball star will come and rip the fast-pitch as long as I do, and I want to tap on her cage, tell her that her dreams will change, that eventually she'll prefer to drink a beer and watch someone else do it. Instead, I wipe the sweat from my eyes, spit on the open blisters, and rage up for the next pitch.

Before I can put my ninth token in, my cage is pitching blanks because the machine hasn't evenly dispersed the balls. The medium-pitch cage is loaded and free-to-use, but I don't fuck around like that. I've got two tokens left. I talk to the attendants, but they are slammed because the concessions served bad pizza. The entire birthday party got food poisoning and shit themselves inside of laser tag.

I rub the two tokens together, sure I could start a fire if I flicked hard enough. I roll my shoulders. They are properly sore but not broken and stiff the way I'd hoped. If anything, I could use a few more tokens. There's a folded five in my sock.

Devon with the still face and brown braid says she'll call someone for me so I return the cage and wait. I pick up one of the yellow, dimpled balls, finger it with clammy prints. Truthfully, I wish they were real balls with rugged seams, but those kind of cages require appointments and twice as much cash. I roll the ball towards the machine. An iguana chases it.

I pull the skin of the blister below my pinky, and rather than tear off as expected, the skin continues to pull across my hand until a red and juicy stripe rips across my palm. I suck air through closed teeth and try to hold the bat but I can't get a swing in with both hands. The attendant still hasn't returned to fix the cage.

The high school softball player whiffs about a dozen in a row and smacks her helmet. It's all about her eyes. She isn't following the ball all the way to the bat. "You're looking too far ahead, but there's no future if you don't take care of the requisites," I tell her. Her auburn hair reminds me of my wife's. Her legs are gold and cut. I get a little hard.

She doesn't say anything to me, but rips the next pitch to the back of the cage. Iguanas scatter. The next pitch dinks off the inside of the bat, close to her hands, because she's a little slow with her hips. I think about hopping in, resting my hands on her waist, and showing her how to properly rotate. The right kind of thrust makes all the difference. Before I offer my diagnosis, my cage is shooting pitches again.

A major league batter has six-tenths of a second to decide if they should swing or not. I might have a full second here at Adventure Zone.

I ponder the significance of those decisions, how quickly a career is made or broken. The softball player watches a pitch go by. I return to my cage.

My tenth token hurts differently. My hands sting, my back burns, but it's dull compared to the ache in my gut. A pitch blows by without a swing from me. Then another. I jump to the right-handed box and the ache is sharper. I drop the bat, take a seat where I was standing. Each pitch that fires past untouched hurts me more. *Fwahp!* They serve beer inside and I consider the five tucked into my sock. *Fwahp!* My palm bleeds slow in micro-spots, a red five o'clock shadow. *Fwahp!* A few of the iguanas gather near me, flicking their tongues with anticipation. *Fwahp!* The softball star leaves without acknowledging me. *Fwahp!* I decide I've had enough.

Gastropod

Lightning flashes sideways and I haul my wife's tin koala from our garage and into the middle of the street. I say tin, but it could be any metal, whatever scraps are made of when artists dig through junkyards and weld enough of it together that it looks like something.

The tin koala (Kansas is its name), is about six feet tall, its eyes made of the heads of desk lamps, and its overall color a collective shade of whatever my lawn is during a storm. A small notecard sits between two claws. I drag and it scrapes across the driveway. Sparks leap like grasshoppers and I take frequent breaks. I stop when I reach the middle of the street. Thunder cracks. The forest at the end of the street grasps west as one. Hurricane Irma isn't quite here, but should be before the next morning.

Near my mail box, two boys bend low and drink rain water as it pools against the curb. They take turns, laughing at the absurdity of their actions, perhaps. One of the boys, round with flat brown hair, taps on the shoulder of the other boy, lean and dreadlocked.

"Be careful. You might swallow a tadpole, and then a frog will grow inside of you," I say.

"Fuck you, Gru," the dreadlocked one says. They both look about eleven and I do look a little like Gru from *Despicable Me,* if only a little more worn.

The rain comes down harder and my house rests like a freshly dead corpse. The light inside my garage flickers and goes out. My Civic beams warm and dry. The back is open, a mound of my shirts stacked inside, glowing underneath the small bulb of my trunk.

"Are you guys hungry?"

The dreadlocked kid looks like he might swear again, but his plump buddy matches the posture of Kansas. There's something appetizing about bad ideas. The sense of immediacy they place on lives. When I pursue a bad idea, my skin seems to fit better around me. The few muscles I have are conscious of the work they're doing.

"What's to eat?" the dreadlocked one says.

"Mexican."

"Shit yeah," the plump one says

I direct the two to the back of my Civic and successfully avoid Kansas as I pull into the street.

My steering wheel shakes and I turn onto the boulevard, sharply, noted by the clink of the bottle beneath my passenger seat. I forgot I cut my seatbelts out, and the two boys tumble across the backseat. More absurd laughing.

The storm is worse closer to La Napolera. The entire sky spins northwest. Wind occasionally pushes me into the other lane and curtains of rainfall blind us for stretches of road. The sun will set soon and it might be impossible to go anywhere, so I step on the gas. The dreadlocked kid is named Chris. The plump one Seth.

"What is that dumb shit on your chest?" Chris says.

I forget I'm not wearing a shirt and my tattoo is in plain sight. "It's a hermit crab," I say. The tattoo covers most of my chest and the top half of my abdomen. There's no real story behind it, other than I like the idea of moving from one shell to another when I've outgrown the first.

"And the metal Koala?" Seth says.

"Scrap art. My wife made it."

"I thought hermits lived alone."

"Well," but I don't finish. It's difficult to find the words that are both accurate and coherent enough for two eleven-year-old boys. Katie is an artist, I can't deny that. So she does artist things. She revels in doubt. She sleeps elsewhere for nights at a time. She tells me my indifference is a virus, one with no known vaccine. She started a fire so she could fuck a fireman. The last time I saw her, she strapped skates to her feet and slung an empty duffel bag over her shoulder.

Another curtain of rain, more sideways lightning. A duffel bag in the middle of the boulevard.

I run over it, the driver side of my car popping upward. More bottle clinking, more boy tumbling. They laugh at the bumps, the way their heads clang against the cup holders. Bugs of unusual sizes smash into the windshield. The rain clears the evidence.

We pull into the parking lot of La Napolera, and there's a firetruck out front, an ambulance too.

"What happened?" Seth says. He's since taken off his shirt as well, stretch marks glowing in the overcast. The boy will be tall one day, perhaps handsome, but not before he narrowly kills himself in the ninth grade.

"Margaritas will turn you into a killer," Chris says, with the pomp of someone familiar with Yahoo! headlines.

There's no sign of a fire, so the three of us hop out the Civic and approach the restaurant.

I was a boy when my dad found out about my mom's affair. He buckled me into the back seat, my older sister Kyle sat in the passenger (she's since died, a belligerent punch on the Brix dance floor. I don't think about it when I don't have to). My dad knew the man my mom was sleeping with, they'd played billiards together at the single bar on the Naval base. He drove us to the man's house, pulled a cheap softball bat from the trunk, and knocked three times before taking the bat to the man's front door.

The boys and I sit on a curb because a fireman won't let us any closer.

"Can we go home?" Seth says, his shirt tied around his head.

"No. I'm not ready for my mom to freak," Chris says.

I pull a cigarillo and lighter from my sock. A firefighter steps to us and smacks the lighter out of my hand. "Are you out of your mind?"

he says. There's something about the way his nose breaks right and I remember he's the one that fucked my wife. He doesn't recognize me because I'm perfectly happy right now. Perhaps the hermit crab is a distraction.

"When can we go in and eat?" I say.

"Not today."

"There's no fire here."

"Sir, there are other Mexican establishments."

I take umbrage to his saying establishments instead of restaurants. It feels deliberate, the posture with which he drags a flaccid hose behind him. The boys stand up, head towards the car, and wait for me. Everything inside of La Napolera is dark except for the occasional flashlight. I see no cats, no smoke, no rubble to sift through. When I'm on my feet, I press my chest, give the crab a little life, but my chest sags these days, my gut melts over my waistband, rain water drips from my belly hair. The firefighter that fucked my wife puts his hand on my chest as I walk past but it doesn't stop me. The hose preoccupies his other hand until he drops it and wraps his arm around my neck.

"Fight!" one of the kids says.

Kyle and I watched my dad and my mom's lover trade blows in his front yard. Fights were different then, a little more dignified. They were missing a man in stripes, sure, and some squared rope, but there was a pulse of understanding between the two. The other man had slept with my mom and my dad had destroyed his front door, his property.

"Make him bleed, Dad!" Kyle yelled from the car, but our dad waved her off.

He managed back-to-back blows, one to the man's ribs and the other to his jaw, and perhaps it was because the man didn't love my mom, was simply sleeping with her, that he lost. I think about this often, the weight of a cause. Where does passion factor in the shape of an action, and is the moment we recognize our buckling leg the moment we've doomed ourselves to failure?

Our dad helped the man off the lawn, exhausted into a swamping compassion, and led him to the broken door. He returned to the car, started it up. Kyle reached for the blood sitting atop his lip and my dad smacked her hand, pulled a cigarette from the glove compartment.

When I told this story to my wife, she wanted to know more of my mom. Why did she cheat? Where was she during the fight? How come we didn't invite her to the wedding?

I'm losing the bout with the firefighter. He's yet to release his hold on my neck, despite my repeated attempts to throw him over my shoulder. In high school, I would have braced my legs, prepared a squat, but my legs do nothing. They wriggle like roach appendages.

A different firefighter pulls us a part. I gasp, choke on rain water. The firefighter that fucked my wife manages a kick to my ribs before he's pulled away again. A gust drops in. I'm reminded how little control I really have.

"Maybe we should go home," Seth says.

"This is not as cool as YouTube," Chris says.

Purple spots the blades beneath me. I don't remember getting hit in the mouth, but I spit a little more and drag myself to my feet. A dog barks from one of the cruisers parked across the street by the abandoned gastropub. The water from the St. Johns creeps into the street.

In the car, the two boys don't talk anymore.

"I've got tortillas at my place," I say.

They search for seat belts.

Kansas the Koala is gone when we return home, removed from where I left it. Water flows, coating the street, into drains. A couple of teenagers try to shoot the basketball, time it with the wind, but miss by a couple feet each time. Two other teens use the top of a storage bin to skim along the curbs.

I park the Civic in the garage and the kids jump out, splash through the yard, and fade into the haze of the storm. A call after them dies before it leaves my mouth. Perhaps I taught them something.

Soon I'm in the street. Through the rain water I can just make out the drag marks from where Kansas once stood, but it could be branch shadows, the sun is just about dead. The shadow marks lead to the garage of Bill and Barb, the seventy-year-old Brookylnite couple we used to drink coffee with. Maybe their son is visiting? How else did they move the koala?

I'm halfway up their driveway and there's this screech. Something like a peewee whistle, but a little more desperate. It only rings for a second. I try to lift their garage open and I hear the screech again, clearly from the grass to my right. A moat has formed around this curved palmetto and in the water a tiny rodent sits perfectly still. Its thin and purple with shut-eyes. I hear the screech again, see that the rodent is a baby squirrel.

The moat fills. I spit leftover blood onto the driveway and it flows into the street. I've heard that you aren't supposed to touch baby animals with your bare hands, so I pull my shorts down and kick them off. Using them as a small barrier, I scoop the baby squirrel out of the moat and hold it close to my chest. Rain drops land on its body. It spasms like a nightmare. It rubs its snout against the shell of the hermit crab. It pulls its own tail into its mouth, tries to feed from anything.

Terra

After my divorce, a hurricane sweeps through and uproots a large oak tree in my front yard. It leans far to one side, its branches piercing the ground, and leaves a pocket of space between the trunk and the yard, something small enough for a cat to die under. The soggy roots pull a moon of lawn with them and leave it ajar, the way the seat of a cleaned toilet sits suspended above the bowl. Muddied water has pooled underneath and inside I find tadpoles, salamanders, and a rusted lunchbox. A scratched football is painted across the tin lid.

In my sink, I rinse the grime off the box and try to pry it open with a fork. It doesn't budge. I find a hammer in a drawer and use the pronged back to jimmy a corner of it open, but the other half sticks shut. It's too early to hassle so I toss it and grab a cold slice of pizza from the top of my fridge.

My phone rings and it's Koby. He wants to bring over breakfast and bourbon and watch the Jaguars game. They are playing in London which means 9:30 start time on the east coast of America. When he pulls into my driveway it's 8:45 and he sits in his car, a shiny foil in his hands. Koby likes to eat Pop-Tarts in his car because the radio sounds better and the bits of exhaust that creep through the air conditioner pair well with the glops of frosted fudge on the side of his teeth. He is divorced, too, but has been for years now.

"It's not carbon monoxide poisoning in the same way that one beer doesn't make alcoholism," he told me once.

My ex-wife left the television and the wireless receiver but I can't find the remote. This seems sufficient reason to dial so I do. She answers out of breath.

"What are you doing?" I say.

"I'm training for my jump. What do you want?"

"Where'd you put the TV remote?"

She hangs up.

Koby drops the bourbon and McGriddles on the couch. I find the remote in a pile of dirty laundry underneath the coffee table.

He surveys my living room. He tosses pizza boxes off the couch, scoops a crushed Christmas ornament from my coffee table. It dangles like a half-eaten apple. All around my house are crushed ornaments, a single clutch each, all in one night. The scabs of my palm reopen every day.

"Let's watch outside. It's a beautiful day," Koby says and tosses the pizza boxes onto the floor.

We pull extension cords and dirty rope from my garage and tie the television and receiver to the drooping trunk of my fallen tree. The leaves provide enough shade that there isn't a glare. There's a nest teetering between two branches. An osprey snoozes inside. We each take an end of the couch and pull it to the front yard. The lawn is still soaked and the bottom of the couch sits loose, bobbing side-to-side as a docked boat would. We eat our McGriddles and share the bourbon.

Around the same time as kickoff a man our age crawls from the hole where I found the lunchbox. He wears a slimed Jaguars jersey and carries a six-pack of something foreign. "You guys see my lunch?" he says and I tell him to check the counter by my fridge. When he returns outside, lunch box in hand, he catches the flashes of the television on the tree. "Shit, you got power? I don't think anybody else does."

I might be the only house that didn't lose power because the last couple of nights people have stood in the middle of my street and watched me through the window eat hot pizza on the floor. They're all wet as can be, arms crossed and faces long. I'm not sure if it's envy or resentment, but it permeates my walls and makes me belch vomit flakes so now I try to keep my curtains shut.

"Mind if I watch with you guys?"

Koby scoots over and the man takes a seat. He holds the lunchbox in his lap and takes a sip of our bourbon. The Jaguars score an early touchdown and we trade high fives.

From my backyard comes a gaggle of teenagers. They carry a deflated football and wear teal bandanas. "Oh, man, is it cool if we watch?" they all say at the same time. Most of their faces are shaded with dirt, Adam's apples swollen with puberty.

Koby and I grab all the dining room chairs and the recliner I keep in my bedroom since my ex-wife took our mattress. I tell Koby we should probably prepare for more people and we dump all the books out my bookshelf. We drop it face down in the yard so newcomers can use it as a bench.

A woman our age crawls from the tree hole. She wears a long t-shirt that says COFFEE ADDICT across the chest. "Trevon, what happened to grocery shopping?"

The man on the couch with us says, "They've got power. Let me watch the game."

The woman rolls her eyes and crawls back into the hole. The osprey shakes its wings.

The bourbon is shot and Trevon opens one of his beers. "She's the best thing that ever happened to me," he says.

My neighbor, Kaila, from across the street comes out to grab the paper, but walks past it and takes a seat on the upturned bookcase. She sips her coffee and smokes a cigarette. She cheers when the Jaguars force a fumble. Sometimes I forget we slept together and it makes me sad. I should think about it more.

Maybe I don't because the sex was sad. My ex-wife had only been gone a couple nights. Kaila asked me to fix her fridge, gave me a beer and a sandwich. It was stupid, really, the way she wore a large shirt and no bra. Her fridge needed a new bulb. When we fell on her couch and I slipped into her, pants around my ankles, she kept whispering "finally" over and over, her breath stale from cigarettes, nipples mangled by piercings. It wasn't long until I was limp and out the door.

Soon my lawn is full. Strangers are happy to sit in the mud as long as they can watch the game. A family brings a backseat full of pizza and Donald from the gas station brings more beer. We drink, feast, and somehow root for the same thing.

At halftime the Jaguars are winning and I see my ex-wife on the television. She's sitting inside of a helicopter hovering over Wembley Stadium. She wears a black and teal jumpsuit. A gold cape rests on her shoulders. The announcers tell us she'll be free falling into the stadium to raise money for charity. If we want to donate, we can dial the number below: 1-800-BAD-IDEA. They ask her if she's ready and she shoots the camera a thumbs up. Then she jumps.

She falls out the helicopter quicker than I drop my beer.

Trevon opens his lunchbox and the power cuts. My television turns black. Everything is cold silent for a while. The teenagers groan and Kaila tosses her cigarette in the mud, returns to her home across the street. Trevon pulls a folded sheet of paper from the box. "She traded my sandwich for a grocery list," he says. He tosses the lunchbox into the hole and takes off down the street. Everyone else scatters like disaster.

Inside I flip the switches of my circuit breaker, hoping it will jump the electricity back but the power remains off. Koby stands outside, beer in one hand, remote in the other. He clicks the power button repeatedly. "What's next?"

My lawn is upended. Bottles float in the surged grass and the chairs lay flipped from the abrupt evacuation. Without the game on, my yard feels like a landfill. My ex-wife is afraid of flying, maybe she wasn't the woman I saw.

I pull my phone from my pocket and dial 1-800-BAD-IDEA. It rings five times and a woman answers. She thanks me for choosing to donate. "Five, ten, or really any numerical value. We'll even take fractions of a dollar. Bitcoin if you've got it."

"Did she make it?"

"I'm sorry, but if you aren't going to donate, we need to keep our lines open."

"I'll give you twenty, just tell me."

"She was amazing. She was a bullet then an albatross. A bomb and then an angel. When she landed I thought there was an earthquake, the applause was unanimous. She never opened a parachute, either. My coworker is convinced she flew. The stadium played that song, the victorious, bombastic piece. You know the one. She removed her helmet and her hair waved to the crowd. We only have a handful of men working the phones, but all of them are in love. Literally. Each of them said so. A few of the women, too. America is proud. We can believe again. Will that be card or ACH transfer?"

I donate fifty with my credit card because I know the jumper was my ex-wife. My ex-wife with the fear of flying is jumping out of planes and I'm sloshed in a swamp of garbage. Koby's returned to the Pop-Tarts and radio in his car. I grab a bag from my garage and pick the bottles out of the ground. I stack the pizza boxes inside and carry the chairs into the garage so I can wipe them down.

Trevon's wife crawls out of the hole again. She holds his lunchbox. "Did he go shopping?"

I nod, though I hope he's run away forever.

"He's a good man. Just got to let him simmer," she says and dips back into the hole.

I untie the television, let it sink into the grass and pull the ropes to Koby's car. He hops out and we loop them through the hitch. When we think its steady, Koby sits in the passenger seat so I can have the wheel. I pull the car around so it faces the street and hit the gas. We reach the middle of the street before there's any tug. The tree slowly rises, a morning stretch. The nest falls below and the osprey flies away. On the radio a Jaguars player has to be carried off on a stretcher. Soon I'm running over the paper in Kaila's driveway. The tree stands tall, though it still leans a bit. The posture seems irreparable. The hole in my yard is sealed.

Koby drives home. I order more pizza and wait. From the window I watch Trevon return with two handfuls of groceries, all smile and gut. When he spots the tree upright, he drops the bags, lets out a yelp. He studies the angle of the trunk then throws his weight into it. The tree shakes but doesn't fall. He throws his shoulder into it again. And again. The tree leans a bit each time. The pizza man pulls into my driveway. He watches Trevon throw himself into the trunk. On one hit, the power cuts back on.

(LOON)ACY

Emerson

a novella

It started sometime in the nineteen-twenties, a bartender says. Prohibition pushed a saloon outside the city, to the no-man's land between Jacksonville, Gainesville, and Tallahassee. Emerson Rogers owned that saloon, and knowing few things as well as liquor, built a small shop on the side of an unused road, spread the word, and waited for thirsty customers to find him. Hands blistered and splintered, boards warped with sweat, Emerson Rogers drank alone that first night. He slept in the doorway and dreamt of a sanctuary for the real American, the wet American, and awoke to the sense that he was lost forever.

Some people drifted by, spread the word, but afraid his shop was too lost, Emerson constructed a large tank out front, fifteen feet long, eight feet tall, and filled it with over a hundred fish of different colors, some donated by passersby. He hoped his message would get across: if you want to drink like a fish, this was the place to do it.

Eventually the drinkers stayed. They built homes along the same road, brought their families, and started businesses. They, too, placed aquariums of their own design outside their shop and filled them with different fish. Not because they, too, sold liquor, but because the investment felt permanent. Lives depended on them. Dante's Café used them as tables and electric eels danced underneath plated burgers. The first bookstore, Page Hopper, constructed tall and narrow tanks between shelves in which jelly fish inexplicably led you where you didn't know you wanted to go. When the highway was constructed, aquariums were built into the concrete sides of the underpass, flapping stingrays could be found at the bus stop, and rainbow fish demanded eyes at the post office. It wasn't until the nineteen-sixties, after the assassination of John F. Kennedy, that Emerson was ever officially recognized as a city. Something about appreciating a thing while you had it.

Emerson Rogers worked as a bartender in Jacksonville before the great fire of 1901 roared through downtown, eating chunks of everything in its path, including Rogers' family-run bar. The following morning, as he kicked at charred frames and swept ash to the side, Emerson resolved not to let absurdity get him down. He spent over a decade rebuilding what had been a staple of downtown Jacksonville, only for the Volstead Act to burn his efforts once again. When the new city of Emerson grew into something of a population, Rogers did what he could to rebuild a legacy he felt owed to him, and remain with as few meddling laws as possible. Drink like a fish, drown in your habitat, because this is what America was meant to be.

HOPE ALL IS WELL, I'M FINE

Xavier chews on an unlit cigarette, sucking on his own spit, and tries to make the most of the postcard in his hands. Maggie, the bartender, continues to explain something else about Emerson's history. Palm trees lean into one another, a sunset exploding behind them. "Greetings from the Sunshine State!" arched in turquoise bubble letters below. It is light and insignificant, which bothers Xavier. This cardboard nothing with the dull four corners cuts the inside of his chest, and he imagines the blood pulsing within to be a similarly bright turquoise. The card could be laminated, at least. He flips it over and rereads the message. Scratched in all caps, his brother's handwriting: *HOPE ALL IS WELL, I'M FINE – C*

Maggie's bar is nameless and humid. No neon signs hang on the walls, the back-light of the aquarium behind the bar is the only thing that glows. Everything is polished wood and sticky from years of spilled drinks. Patrons play ancient pinball towards the back and music detached of theme bounces underneath idle chatter.

She asks Xavier if he wants a light, but he tells her no, that he'd take another beer instead. He's been in Emerson a couple of days now, but hasn't gone anywhere further than his hotel and the bar.

He's spent the last few years of his life selling acres of moon to customers over the phone. It's never felt real, not like when he slid potato chips and chocolate bars across the counter at the Quick Stop, felt the grain of a customer's skin when they accidentally brushed fingertips, but he's accumulated plenty more money. People call in, anxious about the state of the world. They whisper fears over the line, concerns of their grandchildren's surviving adulthood. Some of them speak of the apocalypse, others of the new mating habits between Polars and Grizzlies. The wealthier customers will buy up to five acres at a time, hoping to leave something for their family, and Xavier makes steady commission. Well, made. He's unsure if his job awaits him, if Jensen, his boss, will forgive his undisclosed absence. It's been a dream, selling an intangible idea like lunar real estate in exchange for wealth. No kids, no vices other cigarettes, Xavier has a pretty full bank account and isn't particularly attached to it.

Foam falls over the edge of his glass and Xavier is sure he's made a mistake. Charlie isn't here, in Emerson. This was probably a pit stop to somewhere else, maybe Gainesville, where he slings pizza and dollar Peroni's. Charlie has the dark features, Italian-looking enough to convince fraternity pledges. That's more likely what's happened. Xavier will get drunk tonight and leave Emerson tomorrow.

He inspects the bar once more, looking for faces but everyone in this town wears hats. All he can see are tufts of hair, beards, and shadows above noses. There is an impulse to shout Charlie's name and see who turns, but he decides against it. He's imagined the moment a million times, placed his feet in a particular space, but he could never anticipate the physiology of it all. Xavier isn't nervous, but his throat dries. Maybe it's the beer, but maybe it isn't. He empties the glass and slides it across the bar.

The post card arrived in his mailbox weeks ago. He tried to ignore it, thought about tossing it in the trash, but a longing curiosity lifted the card and placed it on his bookshelf. Instead, he stared at it, studied it, and poisoned himself with the subtext of the gesture.

They were twins, they told everyone, ignoring the fact that the TeBordo family was white and Xavier was black. Their friends thought it was a fun shtick, but there was a sincerity when Xavier spoke. He and Charlie were born on the same day, in the same hospital, only hours apart. His birth mother disappeared, probably between a shift change, no paper work signed or note left by the bed. Their father overheard nurses sympathizing about the poor boy in room 219, and remembering their first pregnancy, one that ended as soon as they learned of it, he mused the idea with their mother. Perhaps the haze of post-birth left her sensitive to the sublime, because she nodded with alacrity, and they took the next steps towards adopting Xavier.

Charlie left six years ago after a gynecologist pulled a still-born child out of his then-fiancée, Sierra. Their parents had already moved to Tokyo to teach, and Charlie disappeared, only leaving an empty room and a note that said: *NOT FOR ME, X.* That was two months before their twenty-fourth birthday.

Charlie met Sierra at the University of Maryland where he and Xavier both received undergraduate degrees. She took a lot of his time and most of his head space, and while the change was an adjustment, Xavier didn't mind having a third-person around. Sierra was like a sister to him, a daughter to his parents, and the bigger his family grew, the happier everyone seemed to be. That's why Xavier remembers the semester before his college graduation as the happiest time of his life. Charlie proposed to Sierra, and weeks later they announced they were pregnant.

Xavier's never asked about his birth mother, not that he expects his parents to know much. The instinct has arisen, occasionally. That's to be expected and he recognizes it before it ever consumes him. What it's boiled down to, is that he's fortunate. He has a family that loves him and he loves them, even if he's been alone the last six years.

He'd never really considered the difference in his appearance. Half of Montgomery County is black and the other half is mostly white. Charlie and Xavier's everyday social time had been just as diverse as they were. But they'd taken a vacation to Virginia Beach the summer of 1992, right before Xavier and Charlie turned seven. It wasn't the way the sand contrasted with his elbows, though he'd noticed that; instead, it was the way his brother tossed and turned later that night, irritated because the sun had burned his skin badly, that carried Xavier into his parent's bedroom to ask them, "How come I'm not burned like Charlie?" They hadn't been out very long, and while Xavier's skin was a little itchy, it didn't redden the way his brother's had.

From what he could recall, Xavier handled the moment well. He didn't cry, nor did he ask many other questions. His father said, "We love each of you more than life," and Xavier remembers believing it.

Charlie walked in next, still unable to sleep, and his parents grabbed the aloe vera from the fridge. They squeezed globs into their hands and rubbed his neck and shoulders. Xavier remembers Charlie furrowing his brow, refusing to look at him.

"Ow! Ow! I'm burned, too," Xavier had said and proceeded to hop and rub his arms.

Their parents called him over, pulled his shirt over his head, and rubbed aloe vera over his neck and shoulders as well. Charlie grabbed Xavier's hand and said, "Stinks, right?"

These are the kind of memories that seem to wade like an alligator below the algae and strike Xavier when he's distracted by complacency. He's felt Charlie occasionally. A sadness will shatter about him, freezing him while driving from D.C. to Waldorf, and an instinct to flee flashes in his brain like some vehement magnetism. This is because something has saddened Charlie, Xavier is sure.

A couple of days prior, before Xavier drove the twelve hours to Florida, sat in front of Maggie the bartender and learned the history of Emerson, he lay on the floor of his apartment, hiding from the cigarettes in his kitchen. He held the post card over his face, and over the top of it he could see the red lighter peeking from the top of the book shelf. Communication had been sparse but at least consistent the first year Charlie was gone. A phone call here, a text message there. What alleviated the pain of his brother's absence was knowing it was helping him heal. But the phone calls stopped. The text messages faded. This was the first correspondence from Charlie in almost four years and it was a post card.

He must've seen what Xavier had seen earlier that week: all-too familiar pictures of Sierra with an exposed belly on social media. She was huge, happy, and according to posted updates, healthy. The father was blond and broad shouldered. Nothing like his brother, and the probability that Charlie had taken note of the common denominator ripened Xavier's own concerns. Sierra wasn't his family anymore, and perhaps Charlie wasn't either.

Xavier thought about burning the card. It could be a clean start, pouring the ashes in the can, or flushing them in the toilet. He could begin anew here in Waldorf, except the only things he ever loved about Maryland were no longer here. Then he noticed a small footnote at the bottom of the card. The orange font was lost in the yellow sunset, but he was able to read: Printed and Sold in Emerson, Florida.

Florida.

He tried to feel the kind of momentum that might've taken Charlie that far south, but he couldn't find it. How many gas stations did he frequent along the way? How many bags of hot fries, how many cans of Arizona did he crush between state lines? When did he know the last stop would be his last?

Xavier grabbed the lighter from the bookshelf, his cigarettes from the coffee pot in which he hid them, and lit up. He smoked a cigarette. Two cigarettes. Soon he was chain smoking in his parking lot, his yellow Ford Escort packed with a trash bag full of clothing and box marked BURIED TREASURE. The smoke of his cigarette swarmed south, he was sure, like wasps traveling for the winter. Xavier checked his phone and saw it wasn't quite midnight. It was almost a new day. He stepped in the driver's seat and put his keys in the ignition.

In his hotel room, a miniature tyrannosaurus rex is waiting for him. It yawns and blinks.

His name is Sebastian, and from what Xavier can tell, this is where he lives. He is roughly the size of a six-year-old child, with a large head and yellow skin. Xavier isn't sure where he's come from, except that he's been sleeping in the room as long as Xavier has. They are like college roommates, randomly assigned, and Sebastian contributes nothing but an uncharitable two cents.

"He's not here. I'm leaving tomorrow," Xavier says.

Sebastian laughs, which means he opens his jaws wide and the laugh track of some awful sitcom plays. Xavier suspects it born of *Family Matters*, if only because it is that familiar.

"Toss me a cigarette," he says.

Xavier tosses him one and Sebastian chomps it down, pointing his head towards the ceiling as he swallows it whole.

"I'm thinking Orlando, maybe Jacksonville," Xavier says. He kicks his shoes off and pulls a cigarette out for himself, sticks it in his mouth and chews on the end.

The walls of the hotel seem stained with time. Thin coats of paint reveal old graffiti above the water bed in which Xavier struggles to sleep. He has an uncle that twisted his testicle in high school because of the wavy support and weeks later had it removed. Xavier still holds dreams of small versions of himself, long afros, no braids, running around the house. Desperate for family, he needs his balls to work.

Broken news speaks from the boxed radio on the night stand. A small hurricane gains strength southeast of Miami. They project it will be a category four before it makes landfall south of Daytona in the coming days.

"Another cigarette," Sebastian says and Xavier tosses him another one.

Next to his bed is the box marked BURIED TREASURE. Xavier removes items individually and lays them on the carpet of the room. There is a sketchbook full of superhero tracings, VHS copies of *The Land Before Time*, a shoebox of unorganized Polaroids (mostly of lizards and unflattering family close-ups), a light-up yo-yo with a knotted string, and a single walkie-talkie.

He examines the items as a unit, a 90s time capsule unearthed earlier than expected, and puts them away, save for the walkie-talkie.

When he and Charlie were in middle school, they bought a pair of walkie-talkies from Toys R Us, and for a while never parted with either one. They replaced the batteries religiously, remaining on the same channel even when they picked up interference from other devices. It was their own secret means of communication, as bulky as the walkies were. This was how they shared their first cuss words with one another, how they talked smack about the other people on their bus, and how they played pranks on their parents. Xavier remembers a specific one in which Charlie hid inside of a suit case. He zipped himself up and Xavier pushed the luggage underneath their parents' bed. They giggled through the walkies, exchanging plans of surprise. Soon their parents noticed Charlie's absence and Xavier pretended to have no idea. "I thought he was with you." Their parents in a panic, Xavier spoke into the walkie-talkie but received no response. "Charlie!" he'd yelled into the speaker. Nothing. What if he'd suffocated? What if Charlie was dead and

Xavier helped kill him? He dove underneath his parents' bed, grabbed the handle of the suitcase, and drug it out into the open, surprised by his brother's weight, how the luggage sunk into their carpet. He yanked on the zipper, flipped the luggage open and found Charlie, eyes closed, mouth open, snoring.

Xavier still thinks about that weight. How the exertion required to pull his brother provided a tangible proof of his existence. But the memory is all he has now, and a walkie-talkie, the weight of which only carries a fraction of that significance. Maybe Charlie still has the other one. Maybe if he keeps it on, he'll find him sooner. Xavier turns the knob on but the batteries are dead.

A convenience store down the street stays open twenty-four hours, so Xavier tosses his yellow hoodie over his shoulders and shuffles a few blocks down. Night time in Emerson holds a buzzing glow to it. Water filters hum from the tanks in each building, and the collective whoosh of a thousand-plus fish cutting through water hushes like the tide coming in. All of downtown sounds like a television never shut off.

As he approaches the convenience store, two teenagers on bicycles zip around the corner, pedaling as though something chases them. They wear emerald hats, triple-cuffed jeans, and black t-shirts. They glide by Xavier, both locking eyes with him, and after passing him, turn around quickly and return by his side.

"We don't know you," one of them says.

Now that they are both sitting in front of him, Xavier can see that they are twins. Not identical, because one has thicker eyebrows than the other, but the same dark hair, rounded jaw bone, and brown eyes. They are tall, too, broad shouldered and slim-waists like swimmers. The one with the thick brows holds a small cage with a still ferret inside. He is the one that spoke. Xavier wonders if the ferret is alive.

"I don't know you, either," Xavier says.

"We know everyone here. We're the Rogers family."

"As in Emerson Rogers," the other twin says. "I'm Eddie and this is Jason."

"Okay, cool. Nice to meet you."

Xavier turns toward the store but Jason speaks again.

"Hey, man. Who are you?"

"Xavier."

"What're you doing here?"

"Getting batteries."

"No, what are you doing here?" Eddie says. Did they want money? "I mean, we don't see a lot of black folk in this town." There it is. Even in the night he sticks out like smoke in the distance.

"I'm looking for my brother. Name's Charlie."

Arms crossed, caps low, Eddie and Jason appear to ponder his question and connect him to the other black people in the city. Surely, the brother is one of the few other black folk in this town. Xavier resists the urge to clarify, a move he hopes is stubborn enough to teach them a lesson.

"Maybe he's the homeboy inside. Dude never leaves that shop," Eddie says. The bikes they sit on look brand new, and Xavier wonders if they stole them. Rich kids seem to like that, stealing bikes. Maybe it's a power thing. The cage dangles from Jason's grip, the ferret apathetic to the tension swelling around it.

"Grab us some beer, will ya?" Jason says. "Maybe we'll tell you something."

The "homeboy" working the counter is a tall clean shaven black man. He dominates the space of the convenience store, his eyes glued to the teenagers outside. His name tag says Malik. Xavier grabs a couple of thirty-two's, a case of something local for himself, and Malik says, "That buzz you hear isn't the filters. I thought so, too. Until a storm knocked the power out. There's something else out there."

"Like what?"

"Could be that portal I've heard about." He doesn't clarify, eyes unstuck from the window.

Outside, Xavier hands the brown bags to the twins. Eddie pops his open and chugs immediately, only to swallow down the wrong pipe and spits most of it back onto the sidewalk.

"Jesus, act like you've been here before," Jason says.

Xavier hovers with the boys for a few minutes, waiting for anything significant. Each of them finish the beer and take turns belching.

"What's your brother do?" Jason asks.

"I don't know."

"Most people around here have jobs. Something that makes them who they are."

Xavier can't think of anything productive to say. So he says, "He likes to protect people. Kills him when he fails."

"Sounds like that faggot, Sally," Eddie says.

"We don't blend well with the heroic kind," Jason says. "But thanks for the beers."

Xavier steps toward the hotel and Jason calls to him again.

"What're the batteries for?"

"To replace the dead ones."

"You're funny, man." He hops back onto the seat of his bicycle and pushes himself the other way. "We'll be seeing you around!"

Back in the hotel, Xavier replaces the batteries of the walkie-talkie, turns the volume knob until it clicks to life, and the familiar red three glows bright. He turns the volume more and static spills into the room, a violent hush, years of things unsaid. If Xavier is to intercept something from Charlie, it will be through channel three.

"This is pretty pathetic, Sebastian says.

Xavier speaks into the walkie, testing the airwaves. "He needs my help," he says.

"This is modern day. The post card was obligatory," Sebastian says. "Had he wanted the attention, he would've emailed you. Sent a text message. Immediacy."

"What do dinosaurs know about the modern day?"

"Ask one of these Florida alligators."

The encounter with the Rogers twins leaves a fuzzy twinge under Xavier's tongue, one he feels compelled to suffocate with smoke. He avoids lighting up until Sebastian speaks.

His shoulders slack, the space where his neck and his skull meet loosens up, and there is a euphoria in letting go. Not because the nicotine has returned to his body, but there is something in the act of giving up the fight. He considers himself a disciplined person, but for the most part he is a pacifist. That's why he bought beer for those kids, why he keeps a pack of cigarettes around. That's why he might just turn the walkie off.

He falls back into the water bed, lets the wave of the mattress shake his head clear. White noise rises and falls from the chair in which the walkie sits. It cuts through the cigarette smoke like a rolling thunder, shelf clouds above a calm ocean. Xavier thinks about what he'll say if he sees Charlie at the bar, or at the grocery store, or on a bicycle. Will he yell? Will he chase him if he runs? He'll probably be stuck, legs heavy like a bad dream, giving up the fight.

"You've barely looked. This is just as much your fault," Sebastian says. He laughs his prerecorded laugh and sniffs the walkie-talkie. A sharp scratch of interference rings from the tiny speaker. Xavier remembers the early 2000s, when they didn't get cellular service in their basement, and would know a text message arrived because the computer speakers buzzed before the phones ever dinged. Xavier studies the hotel room, and anytime Sebastian nears the walkie-talkie, the interference returns, as if Sebastian himself is an incoming message. Maybe he will be the harbinger of Charlie, the vessel through which Xavier gets what he wants.

"I have money, but not enough to stay in this hotel forever."

Sebastian cocks his head to the left, the way trained puppies do when you dangle a treat in front of them. He sits on the floor, taps one claw on the top of his snout. "Will there be cigarettes?"

"I'd like to quit." He takes another drag from the one in his fingers.

"As long as you keep buying them."

Xavier shuts his eyes, imagines a studio apartment above one of these shops downtown. He'd leave the walkie-talkie on the window sill, volume all the way up, and spend his days drinking and reading. Sunlight would slice through dangling dust, rain would leave an after-scent. Maybe he'd bring Maggie the bartender upstairs to admire his pad. Maybe she would see Sebastian, too. They'd find romance in absurdity. But that isn't enough.

No, Xavier needs change. Real effect for a cause he can't let go.

DEAD AQUARIUM

The next morning, Xavier checks out of his hotel and packs his little yellow Escort with the box of nostalgia and the trash bag full of clothing. Sebastian isn't around, nor is Xavier sure how to summon him. Shame, he'd like to say goodbye.

He turns the walkie down low, sets it in his cup holder, and turns the key.

Nothing. Not even a click.

He tries once more with the same result.

Xavier pops the hood and steps out front. He raises the hood up and sees that the battery to his car is missing, a cracked watermelon sitting in its place. He scans the street around them but doesn't catch any eyes, doesn't hear any menacing snickers. An alarm rings within him, but no violence comes. The street is quiet save for the Emerson hum. Xavier peeks at the walkie through the windshield, contemplates the correlation, and drops the hood shut. He grabs the walkie and clips it to his waistband before walking to Maggie's bar.

Inside he asks for a phone and the local police number. "You see anyone trading watermelons for other people's shit?" he asks.

"Got you, too, huh?"

"Wack." The phone rings twice.

"Emerson police. What's the word?"

"Someone stole my car battery."

"Car battery. Give us a dunk and some time and we'll be right there." The call disconnects. Xavier returns the phone.

"Dunk and some time?"

"Don't hold your breath," Maggie says. "Didn't ask your name, did they?"

Maggie pours Jack Daniels into her coffee and rubs the inside of her eye. Her round face and soft nose put him at ease, and her sharp brow makes him feel as though she's always focused on the present. Her skin is much lighter than his own, with tan freckles, but the thickness of her curly hair leads him to believe she isn't all white, that she is some representation of his familial upbringing.

A "Help Wanted" sign hangs on the neck of a whiskey bottle behind Maggie.

"What're you looking for?"

"We need a dishwasher," she says. "We'd give it to a teenager, but the kids around here don't work."

"How come?"

"Just not a concept they're used to."

Static buzzes from his waistband and Maggie glances at the walkie.

"Where's the place to live around here?" If Xavier is going to be stuck for a while, then he'll do what he came here to do.

Maggie disappears to the back and returns with fresh glasses. She pours Xavier a new beer. "There are a few neighborhoods. The Springs, that's the gated community on the north side. The Lofts, those are the apartments around here in downtown, and the Cafeteria, a trailer park on the south end of the city."

"Cafeteria?"

"A lot of picnics used to be out there."

The TeBordo's first home was a trailer in Rockville, Maryland. They weren't there long, but Xavier's first memories click like an old View Master, low-quality still life with crusted edges. He and Charlie had a puppy, he's pretty sure, a small squeaky thing with the sticky fur, but it must've not been around very long. In his memory the trailer is one room (though adult Xavier can reason there were more), with a rough carpet and wooden walls. The smell of empty cabinets still reminds him of that trailer, and he can't really say why.

The most vivid memory Xavier holds is of the tree in their neighbor's yard. The man living there owned a boa he kept tied to a thick branch. The boa would spend all day creeping about the tree, its mid-section dangling from the leaves. Maybe that's what happened to the puppy. Xavier and Charlie lost a kickball in the neighbor's yard, near the tree but not quite next to it. The rule was never to go over there, and while their mother usually sat out front, she'd disappeared inside that afternoon (They later learned in their high school years that their mother had been pregnant and was in the middle of another miscarriage, the details of which they never really pushed for because when you're sixteen, who has time for the undead?). The boa rested high and still, a muscular afterthought, and Charlie trotted over to the ball. The boa struck at him, its jaws un-hinged wider than his head (this part Xavier truly believes), but the rope caught the snake just as it was meant to. The boa snapped shut, swallowing only air, and Charlie collapsed into a ball in the yard, arms over his head and frozen in place. Xavier ran inside, found his mother lying on the living room floor, shook her, screamed something unintelligible, and in a matter of flashes she was wielding a broom in the neighbor's yard and pulling Charlie by the elbow. That was the straw, their parents had told them later, and they moved to Waldorf after that.

Now his parents are in Tokyo, he is in Florida, and he hopes Charlie is too, because he's learning more that he has nothing to go back to.

"I'm trying to find my brother," he says to Maggie.

"This is nowhere." She rests her elbows on the bar and studies him. "I could give you the dishwashing thing."

"He's white."

Xavier thinks of the Rogers twins, how he didn't correct them because hadn't convinced himself it was worth it, but he realizes now that if he doesn't start telling people what Charlie looks like, nobody will be able to help him.

"A lot of white people here. Anything else?"

"I couldn't tell you. He could be missing a limb, or an ear." It is meant as a qualifier, a little joke, but once the words leave him the aftertaste of probability, like a cut in the gum, pools underneath his tongue. He is nauseated by the pain of phantom sibling syndrome, an unaccepted separation, and while Charlie is still alive, does it matter if Xavier doesn't know him anymore? "His name's Charlie."

"I can't recall anyone earless, except Wanda from the bike store, but I know a couple of Charlies. I could keep an eye out?"

"That's really nice."

Maggie pours more Jack into a fresh cup of coffee and pours a second for Xavier. "I'm a bartender and an only child. Always wanted a sibling."

Static buzzes from the walkie, sharp and loud for just a second. Sebastian sits on the stool next to Xavier. He sniffs the bar and the front pocket of Xavier's shirt.

"Are we allowed to smoke in here?" Xavier says.

"Yeah, no problem."

"What's her deal?" Sebastian says and opens his mouth for a cigarette.

Xavier pulls one for each of them. He hasn't seen Sebastian outside the hotel before and is disarmed by the texture of him. In the hotel, the tiny t-rex seemed two-dimensional, a construction paper cutout, but here in the bar, chomping cigarettes with pinball in the background, Sebastian has dry skin; his pores open, eyes wet, teeth a little stained. His yellow skin reflects light from the single bulbs that dangle from the ceiling of the bar. Xavier has been distracted, too preoccupied by his uncertainty to try and decipher Sebastian. Truthfully, he doesn't care for a diagnosis, but now Sebastian has developed shape. A shadow extends from his feet to the floor of the bar.

Sebastian hops onto the bar and trots end to end, tapping his chin with a single claw, and studies the turtles swimming in the aquarium between the top and the middle shelf. Some of them lie still on suction-cupped rocks while others tread water near the top, poking a fraction of their head through the plane of the surface. Sebastian snaps his claws and the turtles swim left, to the edge, then turn around and swim right. Repeat. It's a turtle Olympics and this is the infinite meter swim. Maggie doesn't notice.

Xavier had a stuffed tyrannosaurus as a kid. It was yellow, too, but he never had a name for it. It had been something of a cult favorite, population one, the ugly middle child of all his toys. He didn't play with it the most, but it was always there, rounding out his random and meaningless curation. He'd given the t-rex to Sierra as a baby shower present and hasn't seen it since. Sebastian probably isn't an extension of that sort of memory hacking. No, he is more than likely a creature of a separate plane, a personal anxiety, one Xavier only has conditional access too. While he is curious, the specificity of that condition doesn't carry much weight with him at the moment. His morning cocktail settles in and Sebastian opens his mouth for more cigarettes. Maybe the stuffed t-rex was lost years ago, under Charlie's sea of aluminum cans.

Maggie returns and asks if he wants another drink. "I think the Salamander's real name might be Charlie."

"The what?"

"Salamander. He's the town's superhero. Green spandex, black mask, black boots. He walks the streets, protects the city," Maggie says.

"He's a weird little fucker, too," Sebastian says. "Meets girls at the hotel. Real loud."

"Have you ever seen his face?" Xavier asks. "Without the mask."

"No, but I know he has a beard. Mask only covers the top half. He stops by for drinks sometimes, which seems unheroic, but he's only human," Maggie says.

Xavier reflects on his sketchbook of superhero doodles. It's an interest they shared growing up, but nothing intense enough to warrant a one-eighty of this magnitude. Maybe heartbreak was enough to push Charlie over the edge. It makes for a typical origin story. Dead baby. Lost love. Fresh start. It wouldn't be the craziest thing.

But it feels too easy for the life he's lived.

"I'll take the dishwashing gig," Xavier says and tosses cash on to the bar.

Xavier leaves the bar, cigarettes in hand, and drops them in the garbage. His car sits idle, and he considers buying a new battery. Leaving makes the most sense, but Maggie is a particular kind of nice to him, something more specific than public cordiality. He's happy to remain close for a bit.

"She runs a business," Sebastian says.

"I'm tired of feeling displaced."

The itch to flee melts into an exhausted heaviness. He doesn't have the energy—the emotional momentum, really—to deal with the car just yet. He follows the sidewalk to the end where he stumbles across the bike shop Maggie mentioned earlier. Rather than a sign of sorts, there is a large aquarium above the front door deep enough to submerge an entire bicycle. Lobsters dangle from the handle bars and seat, and seahorses scoot from one end to the other. Near the door, two watermelons sit side by side. Xavier steps inside.

A small woman missing the top half of her left ear sits on a stool reading a book. She blows a kazoo each time she turns the page. "No sales today, but if you buy a bike we'll throw a helmet in for free," she says.

Xavier examines the bicycles that line the back of the wall. Different colors, three-speeds and six-speeds. A couple of bikes have different sized wheels, or even a second back wheel.

"I haven't ridden in a while."

"Yellow one in the front, with the basket," the woman says. "It's fundamental, or some shit like that."

Xavier pulls the yellow bike from the line and rolls it to the front. It seems stable enough. He imagines cruising around Emerson, passing aquariums. He could keep the walkie-talkie in the basket and ride from the Cafeteria to the bar. If he cruises the streets, perhaps Charlie will be the one to spot him.

"I'm missing two prop bikes. You know anything about that?"

He says no and hands the woman cash. She pulls a matching helmet from underneath. He rolls the bicycle out of the store. Outside he spots the Rogers twins cruising down the street towards Malik's. Eddie carries a watermelon in one hand and Jason rings the bell on his bike. "Brothers!" he says, and shoots Xavier a thumbs-up.

Xavier hasn't ridden a bike in years, a consequence of subways and D.C. traffic, and while he hasn't forgotten, there is rust to shake off. The aggressive wobble of the front wheel brings him back to the first grade and the dumpster behind the Safeway near their home. His first ride without training wheels ended with his shoulder banging into that dumpster, his knees peeled like a ripe plum.

He pulls his bicycle into the south end of town where mobile homes surround a large lake. Some small, some double-wide. The Cafeteria is surprisingly children-less and quiet. Geese, turtles, and nutria share the lake, swimming in slow circles without human disruption. Xavier drops his bike in a dirt lot. The interference on the walkie turns sharp, this time lingering for a bit.

Sebastian trots through the high grass, snapping his jaws at dragonflies, and stops at an empty whiskey handle buried halfway in the ground. Xavier surveys the rest of the neighborhood once more, noting the litter of empty handles of whiskey that sit in the grass like fragile tombstones. He steps closer, and able to see into the water, notices groups of nutria, larger than he's ever seen before, creeping beneath the surface. They seem about four feet long, round as a big toe, with pelts as full as kiwi skin. Sebastian pounces on the whiskey bottles one at a time, balancing on a single, clawed toe. He leaps to a fourth bottle and crushes it beneath a weight Xavier doesn't think is real. The walkie-talkie explodes with noise.

Salamander, you there?

The front door of a double-wide to Xavier's right explodes open and out jumps a masked man in green tights.

Xavier grabs the walkie and speaks into it. "Charlie?"

The Salamander raises a walkie of his own and Xavier hears, Where should I report?

There's a rush of static and Xavier is too distracted to decode any of it. Something about the Salamander's shape, his overall carriage, is deafening. He booms where he stands, full moment, and Xavier searches for cover. He doesn't find it.

The Salamander sprints from his trailer and around the lake, pumping his arms, his posture upright. He passes Xavier without regard and continues towards downtown. His dark beard sways back and forth. A tint of green seems to follow behind him. Soon he turns a corner and is out of sight.

"It's not him," Sebastian says.

"You don't know."

"Of course I do." The laugh track plays loud from Sebastian's throat.

Xavier looks to the trailer the Salamander just emerged from. It's plain and unpainted. Rusted aluminum steps lead to the front door. A light remains on through a window. Xavier walks and Sebastian follows.

He checks for curious neighbors and doesn't catch any eyes. He shakes the handle. The door is locked. Sebastian leaps by the lit window.

Through the window, Xavier sees a floor of crushed aluminum cans.

Seven years ago in College Park, Sierra met Xavier on campus. She told him she was pregnant.

"How do you think I should tell Charlie? I want to catch it on video. Do you have a camera?" Her face was flushed, and her brown eyes hung low like a basset hound. Two wrinkle lines stretched from the inside corner of her eyes, not quite making complete bags, and stained her face with a permanent restlessness. Despite the look, Sierra spattered herself with smiles. Wide and genuine. She rested one hand on her abdomen.

Xavier hadn't started smoking yet, so he stuck sheets of Listerine Pocket Mints on his tongue and waited for them to dissolve before responding. "Charlie isn't big on splash, you know."

"It doesn't have to be a big thing, I just want to have the moment. He's been talking about being a dad since he proposed."

This confused Xavier. They were only twenty-two and just two nights before, he'd watched Charlie piss into the truck bed of Joel Belcher, a large redneck kid that'd called Xavier a nigger more than once during intramurals. Charlie was like that, achieving vengeance anonymously.
It usually involved piss and it seemed odd and sudden that someone that peed on things as often as Charlie would be so excited to be a father; though, Charlie's willingness to stand up for Xavier at all costs was probably reason enough to trust his desire to raise another life. Being the first to know gave Xavier a sense of pride and yet he remained disoriented by the news. Charlie was going to be a dad.

"Maybe do it on Thursday? Mom and Dad leave for Tokyo this weekend, and it'd be a good send off." Every Thursday they gathered at their parents, a means of familial maintenance. It'd be perfect. He would've liked to have been surprised with the rest of the family, but conspiracy gave him something to share with Sierra, a treasure he'd remember.

At their parents' home that Thursday, Sierra passed out cards to the family over dinner. Something about showing appreciation for welcoming her unconditionally. Mom, Dad, and Charlie opened the cards at the same time. Their parents, seated side by side, pulled each other close as they studied the sonogram photo she'd slipped in the envelope. Charlie held it up to the light, checking its authenticity, and as the mint strips dissolved on Xavier's tongue, Charlie laughed with a smile he hadn't seen before.

The following six months or so, Sierra's stomach stretched rapidly and Charlie frequently laughed himself awake. Xavier remembered how delicate the moment felt when Sierra explained the story. It'd start with a giggle, she'd said, like an actor trying to hold it together during a funny scene, and Charlie would break, roaring himself awake. His teeth bright in the middle of the night. The phenomenon was both weird and beautifully angled. Maybe it was hindsight, but his family's happiness seemed to balance on a thin branch then, vulnerable to every gust of wind. The further the pregnancy progressed, the less Xavier felt he knew about his brother.

About thirty-two weeks into the pregnancy, Sierra would experience extreme amounts of movement inside of her. Little Jordan (gender neutral and boring, Xavier thought) would thrash about in the uterus, kicking in ways Charlie could only describe as "looney." An endearing sort of violence.

"He's kicking so hard, I can see each individual toe. POW!" Charlie said. He jumped and kicked. "It's like he's ready to come out. We could call him Ninja TeBordo."

But, when they cut Sierra's stomach open and peeled it back to free Jordan, they learned that all that thrashing had been because the umbilical cord frequently caught around his neck. Jordan had been trying to kick himself free. The silence of the birth fell upon them like a switch of the lights. Sierra fell still as well, though perfectly alive, and Charlie disappeared down the street to the one bar with no bathroom.

On Xavier's couch, Charlie lamented that they'd been "fucking arrogant." He stared at Xavier, recalled his comments about "Ninja

TeBordo" and grew visibly nauseated. Charlie bent over, clutched at his stomach with both arms, and rocked in place. "After what happened to Mom, I should've known better," he said and eventually fell asleep in that spot.

Xavier brought home beer and Charlie drank it all. He didn't move for days, dropping crushed cans onto Xavier's floor and soon the living room transformed into the sloshed version of a child's ball pit. Keys, coasters, remotes, hope. All of it lost underneath a layer of aluminum. Weeks later, on a Thursday, Sierra dropped a bin of Charlie's things on Xavier's front porch. Clothes, movies, a Pack-N-Play. They drank more beer and watched VHS copies of *The Land Before Time*, a childhood favorite. "I was looking forward to sharing this," Xavier said and Charlie drooled on the couch pillows. The following Thursday, Xavier came home to an absent Charlie and found the note that said "NOT FOR ME, X." He called his brother's phone and it rang and rang.

He called for three straight days, only breaking for a few hours at a time, until Charlie answered and quickly said, "Let me be," before hanging up. A day later, Charlie answered, but must've ditched the phone in another room, because all Xavier heard was the breath of distance.

Xavier went from having parents, a brother, a sister, a nephew, to having only himself, the orphan he was supposed to be.

Xavier pulls his bike into Malik's, unwilling to leave it unattended. "I've got this," Sebastian says, but Xavier is unconvinced.

Malik is drilling boards over the windows of the store. He shoots Xavier a look, motions towards the bike, and says, "I don't blame you."

He'd hoped to catch the Salamander but Xavier doesn't see him anywhere. A skinny magazine rack is knocked on its side. A watermelon sits suspended between a shelf and the door inside the cooler.

"Did that green dude come through here?" Xavier says.

"Worthless, that guy. Kids steal and nothing happens. No better than the cops."

"It seems like he tries," Xavier says.

Malik shrugs. "If only that were worth something."

Sebastian hops arounds the counter. He jumps at the cigarettes on the back wall but doesn't reach them. Malik finishes with a board and returns behind the counter. A radio plays something broken up from Gainesville. The hurricane's outer bands hover over land.

"Can I grab you something?"

Xavier resists buying a pack. The phantom of the Salamander's presence dances between aisles. The fluorescent lights shine like a laboratory. Between two of the coolers is a tank of sea urchins. They crawl across the glass, slower than success despite their hedgehog likeness. "I'm looking for my brother."

"Not a lot of brothers around here."

"He's white. Name's Charlie."

"I don't know names. I'm here and I'm home." Malik points upstairs when he says this. "Not from around here?"

"Maryland." As he says it, Xavier feels a pang of homesickness. A moment in which he'd like to spot a crab silhouette. "Aren't those kids rich?"

"Not anymore. Not for a bit now."

Xavier asks for the cheapest pack and leaves cash on the counter. He rolls his bike out the shop. The day is dying, the sun already leaning west. For a while he is still, staring at the glass windows across the street, and sees his yellow hoodie draped over a shadow. He imagines his reflection splitting into two—monozygotic brothers—and drifting apart until neither is in his frame of vision. Something vampirical and on the nose. When the indecision has proven too reflective, he cruises to his dead yellow Escort, where he lights a cigarette and sits atop the car. Fruit flies swarm in and out of the hood. He blows smoke, driving a few away, and watches the gray wisps tumble into absence.

Two bicycles ridden by the Rogers twins zip past him. They are in the same black t-shirts as before. "Fuck you, Sally!" one of them yells back. They chug beers and smash the bottles.

Seconds after, the Salamander runs by and stops a little in front of the car. He bends forward, hands on his knees, a walkie in one of them, back rising like the swell of a tsunami. Xavier spots drops of sweat splashing onto gravel below.

"Why do you chase them?" he says.

The Salamander turns to Xavier and stays on his face for a little while. He wears black makeup beneath the mask, making it hard to discern any familiarity other than the color of his eyes; hazel, like Charlie and their mother. He studies their pattern as closely as he can.

"It's not him," Sebastian says.

"Someone needs to protect this place."

"But why you? What do these people owe you?" Xavier's hoping for a clue, a twitch of recognition. Maybe the Salamander will say something like, They took me in a time of need. Xavier crushes the end of the cigarette into the hood of his car. The Salamander watches the flies dive underneath.

"Watermelon in there?" The Salamander rights himself and flicks flies like floating bread crumbs. A stripe of sweat triangles his spine, accentuating the reptile in him. Something splashes in a tank nearby. Xavier prepares for his walkie to fly from his waistband and collide with the Salamander's. Interference burbles from the speaker.

"Want a beer?"

"Beer would be yes," the Salamander says. He smiles wide, teeth white behind his dark beard.

Maggie pours a beer for each of them. Foam spills over the sides of both glasses. The pinball machines in the far corner ring loud and bright. The turtles behind Maggie have dream spasms.

Xavier asks about the watermelon, though he's more interested in the sporadic theft; the demise of the Rogers family fortune.

"Watermelon, watermark, melon mark," the Salamander says. Foam clings his beard like a fungus.

"It grows on the Rogers' land," Maggie says. "Outside that, they have nothing left."

The Salamander gets up and rolls some change into the juke box. Cut and paste hip-hop cracks too loud. More people with hats occupy the bar, but they sit in silence like staged mannequins. Maggie pours them more beers.

In the back, she shows Xavier how to use the dangling faucet and where to place the clean dishes when he's done. It's a small workspace with only two sinks and a standing rack. It smells like bleach and weed. Xavier asks if he can keep drinking and Maggie shoots him a wink. There's action in his crotch and he's relieved when she's out of sight.

It turns into a slow evening, and Xavier kills the dirty glasses sitting in the sink so he can step out and talk to the Salamander. He appears to have a new beer every time Xavier visits. After a while the Salamander switches to wine, stands by the juke box and bounces his hips back and forth. Sweat has consumed the entirety of his green uniform, turning it a shade of forest.

Xavier is sufficiently drunk himself, not quite enough to black out, but a grainy TV snow state of mind. "How many lives you've saved?" he says to the Salamander.

"I don't care to draw lines just yet." The Salamander downs the rest of his wine and pulls at his beard. "Maybe this town should burn, but it's just so wet. It's a stupid boat of hope around here." He belches something acoustic.

His answer hurts Xavier's guts so he returns to the back and proceeds with the closing duties. He returns any remaining dish. He sweeps and mops the floor. He piles the swollen bags of garbage. For a few moments at a time, small tasks consume Xavier's conscious space. No Sebastian. No Charlie. He drinks and he cleans. He doesn't crave a cigarette. The walkie sits in a pint glass, still napping.

From the front, Xavier hears a glass break. He grabs the broom and walks out to find a bobbing man reach for the Salamander's mask. "Music sucks, jabroni." He shoves the Salamander backwards.

Maggie sprays water at the two of them. "Knock it off."

"I protect you. All of you." The Salamander sways in place, eyes on the floor. "Nobody here stands for anything."

The sweaty man pokes the Salamander in the eyes and manages a grip on the mask. He pulls it back, and while the Salamander wrestles with the man's wrist, his drunkenness steers him to the floor. The man raises the mask high above him, a full glass in the other hand, and the Salamander cowers into his arms, hiding his face. "Some hero," the man says.

Xavier drops to the floor to help the Salamander up. He offers a rag or anything else to cover his face.

The Salamander waves him off, removes his hands from his face, and Xavier sees clearly that he is not Charlie. While his hair is brown and his eyes hazel, the Salamander lacks the loaded brow and stunted nose to resemble Charlie. The bobbing drunkard tosses the mask onto the floor. The Salamander licks the hair above his lips and smooths his hair back. "Off to the lair, homie," he says, tears skipping from his eyes. "Time to recuperate." He trips over the power cord of the jukebox and the music cuts. Soon he's out of the bar and Xavier watches him run off to the right. Sebastian laughs at the door.

"Why did you do that?" Xavier says to the drunkard.

The drunkard finishes his beer. He shrugs. "He let me."

After they close the bar down, Maggie straddles a bicycle seat and sips wine from the bottle.

"Wanda said she sold a shifty black kid a yellow bike."

"Didn't know you were friends."

"Beat her ass in sixth grade. Now we stay tight. Got this ride for free." She tosses the bottle back and chugs a large chunk of the wine. "Want to learn more?" She pushes on her pedals and glides forward, opposite the bike store.

Maggie leads him down the main street of downtown. Wind dries Xavier's eyes and he never tires of the aquariums. All of them backlit, humming and alive. Maggie's thick curls reach back to him, an amiable medusa. She turns wide and stops at a concrete structure. "Here's the genesis right here. Emerson's first saloon."

No sign. A dead aquarium. The opening is without a door.

"What happened to it?"

"Time. Evolution. Most relics end up abandoned," Maggie says.

"The same way old people die alone. After '08, this was all they had."

Xavier thinks of his parents, stuck in Tokyo because they can't retire. He thinks of his birth mother, his image of her, and the regret he hopes she feels in whatever hole she ended up in. Maybe it's like the saloon in front of him. He asks Maggie about Eddie and Jason's parents.

"Paris, I think? Maybe Brazil. They're more rumor than anything." Maggie drops her bike on the gravel in front of them. "I dated their cousin in high school. He said it always surprised him that his uncle wore glasses. He barely saw them." She steps forward and peeks inside the dead bar. A squadron of garden lizards march out one of the windows.

Xavier looks into the distance of the opening but can't see far. The edges blur dark, a slow into sleep. Maggie turns and beckons him closer. The walkie spits at them.

"What's that for?" she asks.

"Charlie has the other one."

"How do you know?"

"Because he has to."

Maggie kicks debris away and disappears inside the structure. Xavier follows into the concrete cave with shaved paint on the floor. Broken glass traces the edges where the walls meet the floor and an indiscernible liquid puddles off to the right. Sebastian splashes in it. Shadows blanket the rest.

The walkie speaks again. Audible snow.

"I lied to you earlier," Maggie says. She keeps her back to Xavier and cranes her neck over the bar. "About being an only child."

"Why'd you do that?"

Maggie bounces on her toes. "I don't know the rules about stuff like this. Dead brother stuff." She turns around. "What's the statute of limitations on being a sibling?"

Xavier craves a cigarette. He understands. How much time had to pass until you were alone? Particularly if there was no blood. Xavier because he was adopted, Maggie because her brother's no longer moved.

"What happened?"

"Years ago. I was still in high school. Zane was nine and autistic, but he loved to swim. He ran off one night and drowned in that tank outside."

Sebastian points his snout upward. "I thought I smelt something."

"That's why this place fell apart," Maggie continues. "People here are wigged out easy, afraid to chill in certain spaces. They stopped hanging in the Cafeteria when the nutria came." She wipes dust off the bar and blows it off her finger. "The twins' cousin broke up with me after that. Blamed Zane fore ruining the family."

Xavier surveys the damage. He feels sorry for Maggie. "Why bring me here?" he says.

"He was a half-brother. You look like what he could've been."

They stand in silence, dribbling detritus with their toes and breathing too loud. Maggie's hair casts shadows like Spanish moss over her face. Xavier is almost happy he can't see it, the growing vulnerability thins the air. He's close to bolting. There's a twitch in his calf.

"They say there's a time portal around here. Close your eyes, remember a moment, and it will take you there."

"Do you think it's real?"

Maggie shrugs. "A few people have disappeared looking for it. Octavius, an old friend, killed this barber with his car. He grabbed a flash light and some chips from Malik's store and I haven't seen him since."

Charlie's here. This is why he chose Emerson.

Sebastian splashes in puddles of something gray and filmy. Xavier tosses him a cigarette.

"It'd be nice if it was real," Maggie says and trails off. She stares at the wall.

Xavier pulls the walkie-talkie from his waist band. He holds the button. "Charlie? Are you there?" He walks to Maggie, places his hand on her elbow. "I know there isn't an answer, but it helps to try." He sets the walkie on the bar.

Maggie picks it up, presses the speaker against her forehead, eyes closed. Her hair bounces as she clears the sob from her throat. She holds the button. "Zane? I miss you." She keeps the button down. "Are you there?"

When she releases, interference rushes from the speaker, a high frequency thunder storm.

What do you want?

Maggie drops the walkie on the ground and the batteries fall out.

A shadow stripes them from outside, Maggie grabs his hand, and Xavier spots the Salamander stumbling in the middle of the street. He raises the walkie high, using it to eclipse a street light, and smashes it on the ground. He kicks chunks of walkie to the side, mumbles something unintelligible to himself and continues down the street.

"Malik said he's worthless," Xavier says.

"That's mostly true."

They pick their bikes up outside and Maggie asks if he has a place to stay. "There's a bed above the bar."

He'd planned on sleeping in his back seat. Maybe sift through his shit and reminisce. Residue of her hand sweat tickles his palm. He'd like to hold it again.

"Okay," he says and cruises behind her.

A couple of years after Charlie left, around the time he'd resigned to the belief that maybe Charlie wouldn't return, Xavier wrote him a letter. It was an idea offered by a girlfriend at the time. "I saw it on a television show. You write it but you never send it," she'd said. They broke up soon after but the idea hovered with Xavier. He'd been sick, unable to sleep for more than a few hours each night before rising out of bed and hacking something off-color into the sink. One night, throat raw, he powered up his laptop, opened a Word document, and wrote a single sentence: I am an orphan.

It wasn't true. Not anymore, at least. He spoke to his parents regularly since they'd left for Tokyo, but there was an urgent desperation in the way they asked about Charlie. Sometimes it felt like they were nodding their heads on the other end of the line, waiting for a lull in their conversation so they could ask about his brother.

And Xavier understood, but that didn't make it hurt any less.

He let the sentence sit at the top of the document, the cursor blinking in beat with the cicadas. Then the rest fell onto the page, an alphabet shower, letters splashing and collecting at a plugged drain. It was messy, unorganized, and at times, noticeably pathetic. Xavier struggled with the line between mature adult and reasonably affected person. Emotions were like confidence, there was a specific amount you were allowed to carry on you at any given time, and nobody seemed to know the definitive value.

When he finished it, he printed it out and deleted the file. He folded the pages in half, stuck them in a video case, and forgot all about it.

THE SINKHOLE

In the morning, a sinkhole opens up in the Cafeteria. The ground caves in just behind the trailers on the other side of the water, sucking in all the contents of the lake. The water and fish all disappear into the center of the earth. The geese manage to fly away but the turtles are too slow. All that remain are puddles and half-eaten fish carcasses.

The hole itself is small in diameter, only about a hundred feet, but its decline so steep that the people who've gathered keep their distance. A unique kind of heat seeps from the hole. It rolls like crumpled sheets kicked away during a nightmare, it smells of boiled water after the chicken's been cooked and removed. The citizens of Emerson stand in a circle, all curious to witness destruction. Six-year-olds cling to their parents' shorts and kick the rocks at their feet into the sinkhole. Some of them move like mirages and Xavier is dizzy.

Xavier rests on his bicycle seat. He is happy to be out after wrestling with sleep in the fold-out bed above the bar. He tried masturbation, a post-orgasm smoke, but nothing helped. Sebastian sat on the window sill, moonlight carving a prehistoric shadow across the floor, and Xavier spent the night thinking about Charlie and the time portal. Emerson is too small.

The crowd isn't large, maybe a hundred people. Policemen wave batons and tell people to step back but nobody listens. They wear shades and Xavier wonders if their eyes are closed. He can already see familiar faces; Wanda, the Rogers twins, Maggie, and, of course, the Salamander. He is on his hands and knees, peering into the hole and Xavier realizes that his trailer is gone. Where it used to sit is a congealed trail of mud that slides into the hole. Once the absence becomes noticeable, it hits heavy. The Salamander leans over the edge. "Caroline!" he shouts. It echoes about.

"Someone's had to have fallen in already," Sebastian says. "Tumbled to a dreamy death."

"I wonder if he's here." Xavier continues scanning the faces, bouncing from nose to nose, but he doesn't see Charlie.

"I wonder if he fell."

The Salamander crawls from the muddy trail and pulls himself to his feet. Xavier pushes his bike and meets him away from the hole. The walkie talkie speaks to Xavier in its cactus tongue and he remembers the Salamander smashing his own.

"How'd you survive?"

"Drank too much, woke up in the scooper of an excavator." The black makeup behind his mask is cracked, his eyes scarlet and sharp. "I'm too hungover for this. Have you seen a ferret anywhere? We had this pet ferret."

"Hair of the dog?" Sebastian says.

Xavier spots Maggie gliding away on her bicycle. "A shot and a beer, and you'll be good."

"You might be my best friend," the Salamander says. "But I think I've lost everything." He turns and lies in the mud.

An adjustment rumbles beneath them, something like a heavy door squeaking open. Ground breaks and slides as the hole expands a few feet across. The crowd gasps and shuffles backwards. More heat grasps at the edges and pulls itself out of the earth. Across the hole, one of the six-year-olds slips and scoots towards the endless nothing. From the crowd a white man in a light button down grabs the boy by his collar and pulls him back. Once he's returned, the boy's parents squeeze him tight. The man waves away their gratitude. Brown hair, small beard, a little lazy with his posture. Charlie.

"It's not him," Sebastian says.

The crowd thins and people shuffle to their cars, already bored. Gaps between bodies grow wide but Xavier can't catch a glimpse of his brother. He spots the twins chugging beers and tossing the cans into the sinkhole. He surveys the crowd once more. Xavier pats his pockets and realizes he left his cigarettes in the loft above the bar.

The sky grows gray and quick. Wind shakes dresses and undone hair. Rain falls sideways.

"Caroline," the Salamander says. His face is all purple and lines. "Some hero."

Xavier pulls him up. "Hop on the handle bars."

The ride to Maggie's is slower than anticipated and Xavier worries his front tire has gone flat. Sebastian laughs as the Salamander struggles to dismount.

Maggie's smile is wide when they sit and Xavier orders two shots and two beers. They toss the bourbon back and chase it with the beer.

"I live with my sister," the Salamander says. "I haven't seen her or her moped."

Sebastian laughs and Maggie shoots Xavier a look. She's statued and sad. "What does she look like? Maybe one of us saw her," Maggie says.

"She's old. Got eighteen years on me. My mother was a mistress. Used to own a book store. Dad paid her off and then he and his wife died of age. My sister raised me." The Salamander's voice is even. A few threads have come loose on his shoulder. "She's really small. Smile lines deeper than that hole. She had a daughter a few years ago and gave her up because she was too tired."

Xavier doesn't know what to say so he slides a few quarters in the juke box. He selects some of the cut and paste hip-hop from the other night. He weighs the possibility—probability—that the Salamander's sister is at the bottom of the pit. He wonders how far down it goes, whether lava pops in Florida.

Maggie pours more beers. They down them. She refills. This goes on for too long. Xavier and Maggie catch each other's eyes. The Salamander's head droops forward, not quite touching the bar.

If there is a time portal, Xavier imagines it doesn't work the way Maggie said it did. His own memories are far too muddied, too malleable to be trusted. He's heard before that the way we remember things isn't the way it happened, so could time travel ever depend on memory, when our own understanding might not exist? Time travel could only ever be meta-fiction.

"She's been gone a lot more lately. Sleeping elsewhere." As soon as it looks like he's out, the Salamander pops up and rummages through the compartments of his belt. From it he pulls a small pipe and about a gram of marijuana. "I'm not ready to call a search party," he says.

Customers drip into the bar, gossip about the sinkhole. Xavier takes The Salamander to the loft upstairs. Last night he didn't do much outside of walking between the bed and the bathroom. Still daylight, the room illuminated, Xavier sees more. The floor is an unpolished concrete. A rug lies in the middle, a forest with a napping Bengal tiger. They place a pitcher and glasses on a coffee table and take hits from the small pipe.

"How old are you?" the Salamander says.

"Thirty."

"You ever throw rocks at trains?"

Xavier hits from the pipe. Trains dominate the DC area, but no, he hasn't thrown rocks at them before.

"I've never seen a train. No track in Emerson, but I dream about throwing rocks at trains all the time." The Salamander grabs his glass and chugs the entire thing. "Maybe I should leave."

Thunder growls in the distance like a neighbor moving furniture. It's odd for Xavier to play caretaker. The people around him are emotionally naked, vulnerable in a way that leaves Xavier inundated. His first instinct is to fight the current, find some bearing of sentiment. The Salamander stands by the window. He blows smoke against the glass. "I love the way rainfall looks from a distance. Frozen like a tornado that hasn't learned hate yet," he says.

The walkie-talkie murmurs and Xavier places it on the coffee table. The interference spikes and hushes and Xavier turns it off. "I'm beginning to think my brother isn't here. I thought I saw him, but I don't trust my own eyes." Sebastian rolls on the tiger rug.

The two sit quietly for a while. Rumbles of conversation, the clank of heavy mugs, it all rings inconsequential. The patter of rain and the cackles downstairs operate on a similar unconsciousness. It metastasizes inside Xavier's ear.

The Salamander finishes another beer and pours another for each of them. "First, drink all of this. Second, let's go look right now. Everywhere. This town ain't that big." He pulls the mask off his face and rubs his eyes with beer covered fingers. He clicks the walkie back on. His eyes look like crushed cherries against splotches of black makeup. "I used to use a walkie because it seemed official. That's got to mean something for us, right?"

Xavier chugs his beer. "I'm learning more that sentiment means nothing."

Soon it's dark out. The wind is a tantrum. Xavier can draw a rough map of Emerson in his head. The main street has two ends: the original Emerson saloon on the north side and the bike shop on the south. Maggie's bar rests somewhere in the middle on the same side of the street as Malik's store and the hotel. On the opposite side are the Lofts, a pizza joint, a sports bar, and a grocery store. The aquariums lose their shine as he settles into the town, easing into a familiarity akin to mailboxes or cracks in the sidewalk. He and the Salamander pass the pizza joint and check their reflections in the windows. His hair is a mess, flat on one end due to neglect. His patchy three-day shadow looks thicker in the streetlight. A shifty black kid indeed. Sebastian bounces next to him in the glass.

The Salamander presses his forehead to the glass door. "Caroline?" he says to it. He rattles the door with his knuckles. Xavier wonders if this is shock, or rock bottom. What does someone look like at the bottom? "Has anybody seen my sister?" The Salamander does this for every door they pass until they get to the bike shop.

Wanda sits on a tricycle outside the shop, a small gun in her hand. A cooler rests to her right. It's a blue that's been scratched to gray.

"What's your brother's name?" the Salamander says.

"Charlie."

"Have you seen Charlie?" he says to Wanda. His jaw hangs low, his shoulders slumped forward. His breath is Van Gogh in the night.

Wanda slacks her wrist back, points the gun towards the Cafeteria. "Don't know a Charlie, but those Rogers boys were a little too close. If you see them, tell them the safety's off." Her voice is a velvet casual, but Xavier believes her.

"Got any beer?"

Wanda tosses him a beer, then Xavier.

The Salamander chugs his, crushes the can, and whiffs a punt. Xavier is sure Caroline is dead, resting under a crooked steel blanket, and the Salamander knows it. His search is too standard, a going of motions. If she were sleeping elsewhere, she would have checked on her brother, no?

He thinks about the man they saw earlier. The one that saved the kid. Had that been Charlie, did he already miss his opportunity? If it wasn't him, was Charlie in the pit as well?

"You know about the time portal?" Xavier says.

Wanda nods and presses the pedals of the tricycle. She blows her kazoo as she rides in circles. The thin skin of her half-ear shines in the streetlight. "This girl Devon swore it was in the Cafeteria. She was haunted by an abortion."

Sebastian chases her tricycle, chomping at the back wheels. The lobsters above her claw at the glass, a silent knock-knock-knock. The Salamander paces to the other side of the street.

"Where do you think it is?"

Wanda taps her head with the gun, the barrel points at the sky. The glass of a street light breaks. The bulb stays bright. Glass sprinkles the gravel.

"I'd think those kids know. If there's a time portal, wouldn't their family own it?" she says.

"No, no, no," the Salamander says. He presses both palms into his ears. His beard droops low, weighed by suds and scowl. "I don't have the stamina for that kind of faith."

Stamina, a word Xavier's been feeling for but couldn't quite taste it. He wonders if his years alone have been a carbo-load, a preparation for this Tour de Chance. Or is this the hibernation? Is the ground a fog? He grinds his toes into the asphalt. It doesn't give.

"Where'd they go?"

"Off to the sinkhole, I presume." Wanda stands from the tricycle and rolls the two watermelons into the street. She points the gun at the fruit and after a moment, lowers it. "I don't want to scare the water roaches."

The Salamander runs to a sewer opening on the side of the street and vomits. Most of it hits the sidewalk and a couple of dragonflies hover above it.

Xavier feels his own spins. He catches himself in the window of the bike shop and for a moment, relief descends upon him. His reflection smiles, winks one of its glazed eyes, and Xavier lies on the sidewalk.

All he can see is the dark sky and obese Florida clouds hovering in his peripheral. He closes his eyes. Rain puddles in his hoodie wrinkles. Sebastian hops on his chest and sniffs his face. "Get up," he says.

Xavier feels like he's in the swimming pool back in College Park. He used to spend mornings before class floating on his back, ears below the water, pretending he was deaf and blind. He liked to limit the distractions and get lost in his head. After Sierra told him he was going to be an uncle, Xavier obsessed over a life that he would unquestionably be a part of. His parents lived entire lives before he ever joined them. Charlie, while born the same day, came into the world hours before Xavier was born and abandoned. Jordan, his family, wouldn't live a second of his life without Xavier connected to him. When Jordan was born dead, the disconnect of his everyday life shifted more out of place. Not only did Jordan never breathe from the same world as Xavier, but the bridge between he and Charlie, one that crossed blood, crumpled a bit on one end. Sometimes Xavier suspected it was his own.

Eyes still closed, he sees Sebastian laughing as street lights warm his lids. He hears the walkie's harsh whispers and light dances behind the laughing Sebastian. He sees the Salamander without his mask. He sees Maggie's wink and curly hair. He sees Sierra's large pregnant stomach. He sees Charlie's miserable eyes. He sees six-year-old Jordan with the same hazel sadness. He sees himself, as absolutely nothing, if he doesn't share the pain with them.

A hand grabs him by the collar and pulls him up. Xavier opens his eyes and sees the Salamander studying him. "No time for giving up," he says. His breath is all death.

The rain is thicker when they approach the Cafeteria. Mud slides into the sinkhole which appears to have closed some, but in the dark the bottom is all unwritten fiction. Large nutria huddle in piles on the other side but Xavier can still smell their rank. Feral cats dash underneath steps and grasshoppers leap everywhere. The Rogers twins sit on the roof of a trailer, night vision goggles strapped to their faces. They toss empty beer cans into the mud below and stare at the sinkhole.

The Salamander somersaults behind a different trailer and Xavier follows upright. He lights a cigarette to blow the bugs away. A snake dangles from a lonely tire, tasting rain drops. The Salamander marches with a limp and when they get to the trailer the twins sit atop of, he gets a running start and throws his body into the side of it.

There's cursing above them and the Salamander throws his body into the trailer once more. The dent could be Jesus or an armpit. Shadows and splashes suggest the twins jumped off. Xavier follows the Salamander to the front.

"Batteries Guy, what the crud?" Jason says. "You a sidekick now?"

"You owe beer money, two bikes, the calories I've spent chasing you." The Salamander is all southpaw, and he stumbles to his left.

The twins keep their goggles on. Their eyes are green dots and too wide for their face, lizards in their own right. Eddie pulls a jerky stick out of his pocket.

"In Emerson, it's ours," Jason says. He holds his arms wide.

"Where's the time portal?" Xavier says.

Sebastian laughs. He wrestles with a cracked whiskey handle.

"It's all in your head," Jason says. His smile blooms, corners all symmetrical. "There's a reason no one's found it. You go coo-coo looking for it."

Eddie looks at his feet and then away.

The Salamander balls mud into his hands and slings it at the twins. "Turn yourselves over. We demand a semblance of civility," he says. "Look at that void. Caroline!"

Jason returns the mud-slinging. Eddie scoops their crushed beer cans and slings those, too. Mud and aluminum soar, cosmic poverty, and Xavier finishes his cigarette. The mobile homes around them have hardened in the night the way an empty wasp nest turns to rock. The rain is soft marbles.

Xavier puts another cigarette in his mouth but he can't hold a light in the wind. He chews an end, sucks down his own spit. The mud flinging continues. One of the cans hits the Salamander in the face.

He charges at the twins, stumbles forward, head like a ram. Eddie steps out of the way. The Salamander falls into the mud. It carries him into the sinkhole and out of sight. Quiet.

For too long none of them move. Sebastian looks below. His laugh echoes off the walls of the hole. The twins stare at the hole, too. They remove their night vision goggles and wait for the Salamander to reappear. The wind picks up and knocks them all to their knees. The twins bolt, dropping a pair of the goggles. Wind and rain wipe their shoe prints as soon as they form.

Xavier crawls to the goggles and fits them over his forehead. He moves close enough that he can see the vacuum. He pulls the goggles over his eyes, peers into the hole. Nothing. No light for the goggles to pull from. Xavier crawls a little bit closer, surveys the Cafeteria. Sebastian dances bright, the trailers are statued elephants, and the sinkhole remains black.

Xavier passes the convenient store. One of the boards hangs loose and through the opening, he spots Malik behind the counter, a book in his hand. Rain on the glass warps him like Dali.

Maggie has closed the shop when he arrives. He wonders if they should've boarded up as well. Sound continues unconscious; water filters, rain against glass, barstool across the floor.

Xavier is a frozen wet. He drops his muddied hoodie over a stool and closes his eyes. "I'm ripping at the seams," he says. "Losing in a chronic way."

Maggie's lips touch his, a fresh-baked warmth. She rubs one finger over his eyebrow. He opens his eyes and deflates.

She locks her fingers in his and pulls him to the stairs. He's drained, without the energy to think, so he doesn't. The bed is down and Xavier slides the nightgown over her head. He fingers something like bug bites on her back as he finds the hooks of her bra. It falls to the floor. The wind whistles a reminder. She tastes the way sunburn smells, a crisp sweat. Her hair spreads like a spring halo around her head as it hits the bed and after a while Xavier is distracted by what she doesn't know. This moves like a celebration and he doesn't feel right. "What's the matter?" Maggie says and Xavier realizes he's pulled out. He struggles to start again. "I'm sorry," she says and flips herself on top. Maggie presses her forehead into his, her hair curtains around his face. He closes his eyes. She moves her hips and rocks him like a storm surge. She's warmer than a bath in the winter and the air conditioning has cooled the room around him. Xavier opens his eyes, is charged by the mocha of her skin, and before it's too late, says, "The Salamander's dead."

Maggie stops the surge but he remains inside. She studies his face, then his chest, and continues her rocking. When they finish she falls on Xavier's chest. "It was bound to happen," she says. There's a rapping on the door downstairs.

Xavier wonders if this emptiness is human, or the sign of a coming metamorphosis. He's hollow and warm, an empty cocoon. He stares at the corner where the ceiling meets the two walls and notices one of the lines is off. Whether poor paint or architecture, he can't tell, but it feels like it means something. A dislodged axis. A poor orbit. Something. He slugs his way downstairs.

Maggie unlocks the front door and lets Wanda in. She's an additional ten pounds of water and the gun remains in her hand. She leaves a tributary behind her. The power cuts off and on before the door shuts.

They feed the turtles and light a couple of candles. Maggie pours beer for the three of them. "Why aren't you home already?"

"Stood my ground, now it's too crazy." A drop hovers atop her half-ear. She drops her gun on the bar. "What're these?" She grabs the night vision goggles from one of the stools, slips them over her head.

"The Salamander's dead," Xavier says. "He slipped in the Cafeteria and zoomed into the sinkhole."

Wanda's green dots linger on Xavier. She turns to Maggie and finishes her beer. Her ear and a half turn red. She's full December, tech and Christmas. "What do we do now?"

Maggie refills everyone. She raises her glass. "To the Salamander."

They touch glasses, tap the bar and chug.

Sebastian sits atop the juke box. He kicks his leather legs. Rain knocks the bar in turns.

Xavier lights a cigarette and it reminds him he hasn't showered in days. Maggie smiles to him as she wipes the bar. Wanda takes the cigarette from his fingers and tokes a few times. They finish their drinks. They play pinball. Wanda drops quarters in the juke box. Something fast and jazzy bounces off the walls. The beer fades like a glance. The windows are muddled and silhouettes slump in Charlie fashion. Someone outside yells something unnecessary and Xavier runs to the door.

"You're going to let the storm in," Wanda says.

Rain and wind scratch at his face when the door opens. A yellow excavator rolls down the street. Green dots shine from the driver's face, and another person drinks beer in the scooper. The storm slashes the night, all bad reception.

Xavier shuts the door. He tosses a cigarette to Sebastian. His walkie whistles from his hip. "Charlie?" he says into it. He's chastised by static.

Wanda polishes the glass in her hand and dances to the stairs. "I'll see you in the morning," she says and floats up the steps.

Maggie rights the fallen bar stools. She pulls the plug on the juke box. Soon she's outside, a bottle of wine in her hand. The wind slows and the rain avoids them. The eye. Xavier calls for Charlie once more and achieves the same rugged result. Lightning reveals the clouds.

PEDALING IMPETUS

He wakes in an empty bathtub, pillow beneath his neck, dressed in nothing but his boxers. A candle burns its last few flicks, the smell of clean laundry fumes from the wick.

Xavier crawls out of the tub and flips a light. Orange flakes crust the toilet. Lipstick on the mirror tells him the toothbrush on the counter is his and to make himself at home. It also says his clothes are in the dryer.

He showers longer than expected, the warm water easing the hangover, and he finds his clothing in the dryer. The sleeves of his yellow hoodie have shrunk, so he pulls them up to his elbow. He's surprised the skin of his arms hasn't ripped open.

The microwave blinks twelve and dawn pads the walls of the living room. Boxes of Oatmeal Cream Pies sit one on top of the other on an end table. Posters of old nineties flicks hang above the couch. A small television screen is frozen on a DVD menu, and Maggie squirms between a comforter and water bed. A cat yawns on top of the cabinets.

Xavier checks the drawers and the bathroom but no sign of his cigarettes or walkie. He opens the fridge, peeks behind the television, and drops to his knees by the bed. Maggie wobbles upright. She asks him what he's looking for and he tells her.

"Someone called for the Salamander and you flushed it."

He sits on the edge of the bed and stares at a dusty blade on the ceiling fan.

"We can go to Malik's. I'm sure he has some." Maggie scratches the back of his head.

When he thinks about holding a different walkie, the notion feels pathetic. Nostalgia buoyed his campaign and without it his resolve peels into shame. He's been aimless and naïve.

Maggie brews coffee and lets him stew.

He looks out the window and sees the bar across the street from them. The street is mostly wet and debris peppers the puddles. Wanda slips out of the bar door, gun in hand, and walks towards the Springs. An older woman shuffles between street lights and staples a flyer to the poles. She places one flyer under the wipers of his dead Escort. The car looks to have turned to stone. It's officially morning.

"What do you want to be when you grow up?" Maggie says when she hands him a mug.

"Resolute," he says. "Or maybe a curator for nondescript artifacts. The shit that seems worthless, and probably is."

"I want to keep the bar until I give it to my kids."

The coffee burns Xavier's tongue. He can feel his pulse on the roof of his mouth.

"What day is it?" he says.

She says Thursday and he knows any answer would have been a surprise. Maggie showers and Xavier sifts through books on a table. Most of them are story collections, and he finishes one story by an Amy Hempel that ends with a mother chimpanzee signing to its dead baby. "Baby, come hug," it signs.

A red bandana hangs off the edge of the breakfast bar. Xavier ties it around his head.

Maggie meets him at the table steamed fresh. A head band pulls her hair out of her face and she is beautiful. Her freckles look like beach pebbles below polished marbles. She asks if his memory has cleared up.

Xavier can only remember spots. Passing the bottle of wine. Burying it under some mud. Pissing by a pay phone. He remembers Maggie never told him no. If he wanted to look for Charlie in a ditch full of water, then he was free to jump in. He can't remember if he did. He's certain he cried in her chest. He's retroactively embarrassed. He remembers climbing the steps to her loft on all fours.

He remembers the gazebo with the Christmas lights plugged into a generator. He remembers skipping into nothing before they turned back to Maggie's. The rain cut his face and Maggie ran past him. Behind them was the buzzing hum of water filters. Ahead of them was mud and night forever until he saw the glowing gazebo. He remembers sitting inside, seats rotten with wet, and thinking of the day Sierra told him he was pregnant. In the middle was a flooding fountain. A cardinal tipped its beak into the water and Xavier spotted two stained eggs submerged in the fountain. Sebastian tried to eat the bird. He remembers feeling time rewind around him.

He asks Maggie if they ever saw Charlie and she says no. They sit quietly and finish their coffee.

"I really thought we found the portal." But he doesn't mean it.

Maggie hold his hand across the table. "Where do you want to start today? "We haven't been to the Springs, yet," she says. "He could be anywhere."

He squeezes her hand. They put the mugs in the sink. Xavier pulls her close and leads her outside.

The sun stabs at the world. The wind soars down streets and alleys. The flyer under his wipers calls for a missing ferret. Xavier opens his car and reaches into the cardboard box. From it he grabs the VHS copy of *The Land Before Time*, opens it, and pulls the letter he wrote years ago. He slips it into his back pocket, sure to dispose of it later. Inside the bar, he tapes the flyer for the missing ferret to the front door.

Maggie settles in behind the bar and Xavier rinses the few dishes from the night before. They get the juke box going. He sprays her with the hose. She whips him with her rag. Xavier plays pinball and does his best to plan nothing. Hardly remembering last night, he wants to be present. Short-minded as the days of his youth, instinctual as driving through a fog. Some days, the morning feels ready for change.

People accumulate in the bar. Some of them have leaves in their hair, dirt on their faces. They've been cleaning all morning, they say. A woman comes in with Christmas lights wrapped around her arm. Xavier asks her where she found them and she tells him they were tossed in the mud near the Cafeteria.

The door remains open and soon there are more people than glasses. Xavier's happy to rinse and repeat because Maggie makes him feel like this version of him, the orphaned one, is a perfectly fine version to be. His condo in Waldorf waits for him, stale and untouched, but he doesn't want it anymore. He likes what she said about giving the bar to her kids.

"You don't know what you want," Sebastian says from a mop bucket.

Xavier points the hose at him and sprays water on the wall.

He takes a tray of clean glasses to the front. The old woman with the flyers sits at the bar. A small woman, eyes dark and face cut with wrinkles, she bounces for his attention.

Xavier pours a beer and slides it to her.

"No, thanks," she says. "I'm just wondering if you've seen someone."

"Twins had a ferret, but that was days ago," he says.

"The Salamander. Green tights. Black mask." Her bottom lip flicks against her front teeth. "I'm his sister." Her eyes reach for him, but can't escape her grasping crow's feet.

A skinny dude in a pizza shirt grabs her beer. "Not in a couple of days," Xavier says. He carries a bin of dirty glasses back, rinses them and returns to the front. Mostly everyone has a beer. The juke box plays the cute and paste hip hop. The Salamander's sister repositions her dry bun atop her head. She hovers near the bar like a dragonfly, her eyes glued to Xavier.

"Tell her he's dead," Sebastian says. Someone nearby lights a cigarette and he trots over, laughing his tracked laugh. "Tell her you know all about dead brothers."

Xavier pours himself a drink, downs it.

The Salamander's sister leaves her remaining flyers on the bar and walks out. The other night flashes and Xavier remembers her name is Caroline.

Wanda walks in and Xavier tosses her a rag. He tells Maggie he'll be back.

Caroline is quick. Her small feet chug beneath a long skirt and she hooks a left at the end of the street. Xavier grabs his bicycle, Sebastian in the basket, and pedals after. When he turns the corner he spots Caroline balanced on a moped. She starts the motor and zips around another corner and onto a dirt road. Xavier follows.

She leads Xavier miles past marsh and uprooted trees. They pass the gazebo from the night before and the mundanity is booming. The moped zips around a few heavy puddles and Caroline stops at fallen gate. Xavier drops his bike behind a curved palm tree and waits. Half-buried VHS tapes lead her to a double-wide trailer with a Siamese tree and two-foot garden gnome. A small tank sits below a window. Baby monitor lizards rest on suction-cupped rocks. A few dive in when Caroline knocks twice and disappears inside.

Sebastian bounces atop the VHS tapes. A watermelon rots by the tree. Xavier walks the steps.

"Don't," Sebastian says.

"Why not?"

"You don't need the responsibility. Your inaction would be perfectly Shakespearian."

Xavier agrees but he knocks twice. The door feels thin, like those of his old office. It opens and he's greeted by the tip a shut umbrella. Behind the door, his brother Charlie grips the handle, a small girl with dark hair clings to his pant leg.

Two couches sit against opposite walls facing one another. An automatic air freshener spits every ten minutes from the window sill behind Charlie's couch. They sit facing each other. The small girl kicks her legs next to him. She's got the same eyes as the Salamander, and coincidentally, Charlie.

"I like the headband," Charlie says after a while. He's much heavier than the last time Xavier saw him. Bearded as always, though that's thicker too. He wears a faded black t-shirt, the University of Maryland crab cracked in the middle. Atop his head is a plain khaki ball cap.

Caroline brews coffee in the kitchen. Charlie asks her if she's had any luck.

"He says the Rogers kids have Gus."

"You're kidding. What about your brother?"

She doesn't answer.

"Who is this?" Xavier asks. The little girl squeezes Charlie's arm. She pushes her face into his shoulder.

"This is Aubrey. My daughter," he says, and kisses the top of her head. To her he says, "Can you go help Mrs. C in the kitchen?"

Aubrey scoots herself off the couch and hops through the doorway. She smiles the whole way and Xavier's sure she isn't real.

"Let's head to the back."

Charlie's bedroom is simple and musky. A bottle of unopened bourbon sits on a small dresser. A made waterbed is pushed against a window, stuffed with an old air conditioner, and a reading chair sits at the end. The floor creaks and Xavier is careful with his steps. He takes a seat in the chair and is still. Charlie bobs on the bed and stares at the wall. They are quiet until Xavier feels like he may pass out.

"Who's the mother?"

"Long story, but Caroline. She didn't want her, and I was here."

Xavier remembers the Salamanders' remarks in Maggie's bar. "Why is she here now?"

"I couldn't tell you. Showed up a couple weeks ago. Said she was having nightmares."

No pictures hang on Charlie's walls. They are barren, save for a shallow dent above the light switch. Change, books, and folded laundry cover the dresser. The floor is clean. Empty pudding cups rests on the nightstand. The presence of beige haunts the room. He doesn't recognize anything and without a memento to calm him, he stands. "I thought we were brothers."

Charlie reaches for him and Xavier steps away.

"I couldn't stay," Charlie says. His voice quiets then, words squeaking their way from his throat.

The tepidity of it pisses Xavier off. Be resolute! he thinks. Own your choice! He finds himself shaking his head, eyes closed, and when he opens them his arms are around Charlie, attempting to pull him down. They grapple one another as amateur wrestlers and fall to the floor. Xavier drives his fists in Charlie's ribs and Charlie presses a hard palm into Xavier's face. They rumble and reposition. Xavier throws an elbow in Charlie's back. Charlie flips Xavier over and into a headlock. More squirming and both are free and on their feet. They crouch. They raise their hands. Their breath is heavier than their resolve. Years of smoking seethe from within.

"Six years is eight pregnancies. Imagine it," Xavier says.

Charlie's jaw droops and he makes face like he's just woken up. Xavier is sorry for what he said but doesn't voice it. The points between hugging, punching, and bolting are all Bermuda. The speed in which the rest of the world doesn't matter is disorienting, and Xavier finds no signs of safety.

His brother falls back onto the bed, rocks back and forth. He covers his face and blows air between his fingers. "At one point it seemed too long. Before I knew it, sadness turned to shame. I don't know what else to say."

Aubrey calls for Charlie from the hallway. He stands, rests a hand on Xavier's shoulder. His face is scarlet from their fight. Xavier shakes him off.

"Hang around. If she's taught me anything, all messes can be cleaned."

In the living room, Aubrey somersaults to applause. Caroline leans against the kitchen doorway. Her gaze shoots the distance. The guys return to their mirroring couches.

"You know, Xavier here is my brother." He says this while looking at Xavier. "We're twins."

Caroline looks to Charlie, then Xavier. "I don't think so," she says.

"Brother?" Aubrey says. She brushes her hair out of her face. "Who's brother?"

"My brother," Charlie says. "This is your Uncle X."

Aubrey somersaults across the floor and crosses the rug to Xavier. She kisses his knee cap. "I love you!" she says and disappears into a bedroom.

Xavier feels flattened, pinned in place. The happiness he's prepared for hasn't come. Rather, he's bewildered, displaced in a dreamscape. He swallows his spit, clicks his tongue. He is conscious with his breaths, but as he peeks around the corners of this trailer, nothing pulls him away. The smell of coffee crawls from the kitchen. The moment is aggressively present.

"It's like I found the portal," Xavier says. "A rip in the continuum."

Charlie laughs. "Doesn't exist. I heard it was in the Cafeteria once." He scratches his beard with both hands, something he's always done. "But this is a trip."

Xavier wishes he had a beer, or his cigarettes. His hands are clammy against the ribbed corduroy couch. His stomach is gnarled and tight. "I'm an uncle."

"That you are." Charlie opens the window, drops food to the monitor lizards below.

Aubrey returns, face scrunched and red. "I forgot they stole my Gio!" Tears dive into the corner of her mouth. She thrashes about the floor.

Charlie pulls her into his lap and holds her close to her chest. "Daddy was waiting for the storm to pass," he says. Aubrey's despair feels heavy and real. Xavier is envious and nostalgic for the times his emotions were as binary. Solutions used to be translucent. Charlie asks Caroline if she'll watch Aubrey for a bit. "Want to help me with something?" he says to Xavier.

Xavier isn't sure, but he follows him out the door.

Charlie rides the moped and Xavier pedals after him to the Springs on the other side of town. It's a gated complex but the storm blew the call box and the gate is left open. Homes are separated by fifty yards of grass. Sorted piles of leaves dot most of the lawns except for one. This is where they stop. Tire tracks extend from the driveway and wrap around the side of the house. Charlie parks the moped and Xavier drops his bike. Leaves crack beneath their feet.

"I wish he wasn't so clean," Sebastian says. "At least be a drunk, something. Heroin could've been fun."

Charlie isn't much taller than Xavier, never was, but he looms more adult now that he's standing. His beard is a forest. His back is a wall. He rattles the front door of the house. Nobody responds. Charlie knocks again and they smell smoke.

They follow the tracks in the grass around the house and spot a yellow excavator parked next to a wide fire pit. Jason sits in the scooper, covered in empty beer cans, and tosses old toys from a trash bag into the flames below. He's just tossed an RC helicopter in when he spots them in the background.

"Batteries Guy. Sir Charles."

"Where's your other half?" Charlie says.

"Bitched out. Went job hunting," he said. Jason finishes another beer and tosses a knotted slinky into the pit. "It's like someone never taught him loyalty."

Before he can grab another toy Charlie has him by the shirt and is pulling him out of the scooper. He turns the trash bag over. A plastic dump truck, a GI Joe, some jacks, a couple hacky sacks, and three of the four Ninja Turtles fall to the grass. Charlie isn't satisfied. "Where's my daughter's Gio?"

Jason looks to the pit and back to Charlie. "I've been drunk for weeks, man."

"Think he'll throw him in?" Sebastian says. He peeks into the pit and laughs.

"If you tossed it," Charlie says and pulls Jason through the back door of the house.

They are gone for a good bit and Xavier spots the rows of vines behind the excavator. They extend the length of a football field, sagged and unkempt. Birds dive in and out of the rows. Few of the watermelons seem to have survived the storm. Red guts cover the leaves like autumn. More toys and junk litter the leafy paths. A couple of bikes lay flat amongst the fruit. More empty bottles and cans reflect fresh sunlight. A car battery is seasoned with playing cards. Xavier means to grab it but he spots an old stuffed tyrannosaurus rex. His old stuffed tyrannosaurus rex. Its yellow has faded into a cream but he knows it's his because a black X crosses the stomach. It's crusted with age. The mouth is stitched shut but he sees an upward curve he doesn't remember being there. He squeezes it once and Charlie storms out of the house.

He holds Jason by the back of the neck and carries a caged ferret in the other hand.

"Is this the Gio?" Xavier says.

Charlie smiles and shoves Jason forward. "Let's get out of here."

Jason scoops the hacky sacks and hops back into the scooper. He cracks open a new beer and tosses the hacky sacks into the pit one-by-one.

Back out front, Charlie holds the t-rex in front of him. "Brings you back, huh?"

The hollowness of the Rogers' house looms in the shadows cast by the creeping sun. If Jason is alone, how long until he burns it all down?

Xavier asks if they can stop by the bar and Charlie's happy to extend his tiny vacation.

"I love the girl, I do, but she doesn't crash. She's all bounce and micro naps," he says.

Spots of broken glass and a few fallen stools cover the floor when they walk in. The juke box is skipping. Wanda sits lotus on the bar with a bottle of wine nestled in her crotch. One of her sleeves is torn at the shoulder. She says Maggie's upstairs looking for more wine, that a large fight just finished between two groups of men. When they ask over what, she tells them the debate between laser tag and kickball as an American pastime turned passionate. One man wearing laser tag equipment pulled his gun and shot the laser in another man's eyes. His friend produced a kickball and hit the gunman in the face. She pulls one of Caroline's flyers from a pile next to her. "Is that this ferret?"

"This is my brother. Charlie," Xavier says.

Wanda studies the two of them. "America," she says, and sips the wine.

Maggie comes down with two more bottles and kicks the jukebox into smooth serenade. She hugs Charlie following their introductions and the four of them pass the open bottles. There's a jubilance in the way Maggie speaks to Charlie, and Xavier is floored by happenstance. Luck made him a TeBordo and anxiety carried him to her. He's tearing at the seams again. This fortune bears foreboding.

"I haven't had wine in years," Charlie says. "I fall asleep too early."

Xavier takes the bottle from him because he has questions. Did he come to Emerson for the portal? Initially. Did he look for a long time?

No. How did he meet Caroline? She came into his shop. What shop? The pizza joint by Wanda's store. Did he know the Salamander? Only by mask. Did he miss the family? Of course. Why didn't he call? It never felt the right time. Did he talk to Mom and Dad? Once, but he couldn't bear the magnitude of it. Why'd he send the post card? He liked the fragility. Why Aubrey? Because he knew one in college, and the distant familiarity softened the strange of Emerson. Did he still have the walkie-talkie? He gave it to Caroline because the Salamander refused a cell phone. Anything else Xavier should know? Charlie and Wanda slept together a few years back but Wanda doesn't remember it.

"I was skinnier then," Charlie says.

Xavier holds the stuffed t-rex in front of him. "I thought this was lost in Maryland."

"She loves him. Tries to feed him sticks."

Eddie steps in wearing a polo. He holds a resumé, hand-written on a brown shopping bag. He spots the ferret on the bar and looks down at his feet.

Maggie ignores him, but Wanda takes it, looks it over. "You're practically illiterate, but if you bring my bikes back, you're hired."

He nods too much and steps out the bar.

They stay until it's dark and the wine is done. Maggie trades the moped keys for the Missing Ferret flyers, so Xavier and Charlie head out on foot. Xavier opens his car and grabs the box of junk from the back seat. Before they make the turn towards the nothing and Charlie's home, Xavier asks if they can stop by the Cafeteria first. He worries the moment Charlie returns home is the end of their reunion.

The Cafeteria is a dry droop when they arrive. With no wind or rain it feels like a monument. All that's missing are flood lights and a history lesson. He carries the box to the trailer from the other night and sits between it and the sinkhole. The hole itself is a still anticipation. Grasshoppers leap into it. When the wind does come, a heavy echo bellows like blowing into a glass jug.

Xavier opens the box and unpacks the contents. He lays them in a straight line. The VHS tapes, the sketchbook, the knotted yo-yo, the box of Polaroids. In the box he finds an old pack of cigarettes and a lighter. He sits the stuffed t-rex in front of them. Xavier hopes to jog a raw repentance from Charlie.

Sebastian marches up and down the line. He spits on each item before moving on to the next.

"The Salamander fell in and I didn't tell Caroline," Xavier says. "That's how I found you." It feels selfish and unsatisfying.

Charlie pulls a few Polaroids out of the box. There's the two of them when they were eight, wearing matching Orioles jerseys. He flips until he comes across one of him and Sierra, seated close together at Ben's Chili Bowl.

"I know disappearing was wrong, but I can't imagine myself anywhere else," he says.

Charlie takes the lighter from Xavier, lights the corner of the Polaroid and lets it burn for a while before tossing it into the sinkhole. Sebastian chases it and avoids falling over the edge. He grabs another Polaroid and repeats.

The flicker of the lighter cuts through the high frequency ring of an empty night. It's the only thing that feels real to Xavier. Charlie raises the lighter to three Polaroids at once and the flame grows greedy and bright. Shadows dance against his hardened face. He tosses it into the hole before it licks his fingertips. They watch it fall, casting unsure shadows until it disappears. He holds the box to Xavier.

"You do it," he says.

Xavier pulls one of he and Charlie dressed as Power Rangers holding lumpy pillow cases. He flicks the lighter, watches the flame whip the frame into a crinkle and tosses it into the hole. They take turns, burning several at a time. Xavier is addicted. Each toss alleviates something sharp, a softening sobriety. Sebastian chomps at the small balls of fire. He licks the smoke and laughs at the gesture. Charlie grabs the VHS tapes, breaks them open, pulls the film, and lights it next. He punts the hard plastic casing into the hole. The sketchbook follows, individual drawings crumpled and burned. The yo-yo won't stay lit so Xavier tosses it as high as he can and they watch it soar like a flaccid meteor. They ball the flyers and toss those, too.

Xavier wants more so he empties his pockets. He pulls a business card from the hotel, some napkins from Maggie's bar and the letter he wrote to Charlie long ago. He lulls over handing it to him, but rides the cleanse. He lights that as well and tosses it in.

All that remains is the stuffed t-rex. They kick the box into the sinkhole. Xavier holds the t-rex up to his face. Its black eyes are glassed like a blind man. He presses his thumb into its stomach. He remembers tying the t-rex to his bedpost at night so it wouldn't ever leave. He remembers Sierra's smile when she unpackaged it from a gift bag, understanding what the gesture meant to Xavier.

Charlie pulls the t-rex from Xavier and appears engaged in his own reminisce. He flicks the lighter and touches it to the t-rex's tail. The flame is a slow climb, reaching and pulling. Charlie sets the t-rex down, upright in the mud.

"What about Aubrey?"

"Next week she'll have a new toy. Her memory is a fleeting survival." The t-rex burns and Charlie smiles. "We could learn a lot from her," he says. He grabs the ferret and leads Xavier away from the Cafeteria, back to their original path. "I'll tell Caroline about the Salamander."

Away from the Cafeteria, Xavier looks back and spots a faint silhouette dancing against the long side of a trailer. Next to it, he sees the shadow of Sebastian, licking its wounds.

Xavier decides he should tell Caroline what happened to the Salamander

"Are you sure?" Charlie says. "This is heavy."

He is sure. There's an impetus pedaling within since they left the hole. It isn't euphoric, no, but something softer. When they reach the trailer, Xavier finds himself marching forward, almost skipping. Anxiety turned adrenaline.

Inside, Aubrey naps on a couch. Charlie sets the ferret on the coffee table. He scoops Aubrey and carries her to bed. Wind shakes the ends of his trailer. Caroline sits on the opposite couch, eyes shut. She stirs as they enter and rolls into a more comfortable position. Her peace is palpable and the fragility is intoxicating. Xavier shuts his eyes and covers his ears. When he speaks, he is underwater.

"Your brother died. He slipped in the storm and fell into the sinkhole," Xavier says. "I'm sorry I didn't tell you before."

Xavier waits for something to be thrown, but he measures no agitation. He opens his eyes.

Caroline stands from the couch. She stares at the ceiling, eyes leveled, and Xavier fears she's about to deflate into a bag of skin. The ferret's restless roll is the loudest sound in the trailer. Caroline blows air at her nose, bites her lip. The gorges of her smile lines contort into a hieroglyph of despair. She bends forward, head almost level with her waist, and moans. It's an octave too low and Xavier thinks she might die. She grabs the ferret, and steps out the front door. Through the window, he watches her walk through the broken gate, around a fallen tree, and into the black.

The pedaling impetus is gone. It's replaced by an implosion of the gut. Charlie returns to the living room, drops a hand on Xavier's shoulder and Xavier falls into his brother. He wails and he shudders, and Charlie holds him tight.

"That was big. That was big," he says.

They move to the couch and don't say anything. Charlie bites his nails. Xavier stares at the window across from them. Their reflections are translucent, backlit ghosts of an old habit. Inside, next to his brother, it's hard to differentiate between Florida and Maryland. He knows he's elsewhere, that 760 miles bridge him and his upbringing, but the differentiation is ironed by the presence of Charlie. Xavier allows himself to fall over and rest his head on Charlie's shoulder. The pace of his breath evens his own.

Soon Charlie's eyes betray his posture and he's asleep.

Aubrey calls for her dad to come to the bedroom. She says she misses her Gio. Xavier stares down the short hall, spots the shades of movement underneath a door, and slips out the trailer.

Maggie's locking up the bar when Xavier arrives and seeing her fans the fog that carried him there. The subsequent manifests into possibility, a reasonable acquisition, if not immediate. Xavier is low, but that's why the first steps feel so productive.

He follows Maggie back to her place. They fall into the water bed, hands locked.

"She demanded the keys and zipped away on the moped," Maggie says of Caroline. "I've never seen someone so close to oblivion."

Xavier is quiet, imagining the obtund painting of grief. The bed rocks him into recollection.

"You found him," Maggie says.

Death has slowed Emerson down, and he's desperate to take advantage. His rest is deliberate. He and Charlie shared a room growing up. Later nights, when girlfriend anxieties and existential insects buzzed behind their eyelids, the two partnered up to pass the night. They played cards, drew caricatures of friends, and gave each other jagged mohawks. The hum of Emerson's filters reminds Xavier of their cheap clippers, how the buzz plucked at the nerves inside his ears. When they finished the haircuts, their hair blended together on the bathroom floor. Xavier's mohawk stood unchallenged, Charlie's flopped to one side.

"Was he the same?"

"Something's different, but it could be me. It's like finding an old toy in the back of a closet. You remember it, but the experience is a little off," Xavier says.

"That's not a bad thing, to be different than kid-you."

Xavier's not sure he agrees. He sits up in bed, brings his knees to his chest. "I don't want to have a nightmare."

Shadows of passing pedestrians cover the walls of Maggie's loft. She rolls out of bed, glides to the kitchen, and prepares a pot of coffee. She pushes a tape into her VCR, and a film Xavier hasn't seen, but recognizes, plays. It's an old version of *Macbeth.* He can't remember the last time he watched a movie, much less with another person.

In the trailer, Charlie sat to the left of him, and here in the loft, Maggie sits to his right. A human timeline in which he can't experience both past and present at once. The duality pulls Xavier's mind from the present, but the coffee eases his exhausted anxiety.

"Is this the kind of place people can stay?" he says.

"Everyone wants to leave, I think. But there's a reason they haven't."

"How come you didn't go?"

Maggie digs her fingers into her stomach, pulls on a layer of fat skin. "Magnetism isn't the right word, but my gut is anchored in that bar," she says.

Tomorrow, and tomorrow, and tomorrow, Macbeth says from the television.

Xavier resigns himself to sleep. If he has a nightmare, so be it. At least he will wake up.

An hour later, he's wide awake again. He slips from the bed and leaves Maggie's apartment.

The yards of the Springs are a street-light orange. Xavier keeps his yellow hoodie over his head. When he reaches the twins' home, all the lights shine through the windows. He can see bottles stacked on top of a coffee table. A few of the pictures on the wall look cracked and smashed.

Xavier makes his way to the backyard and grabs the car battery he spotted the day before. Some of the cards stick and he peels them off. He isn't sure if the storm killed the battery, but he sees no harm in giving it a try.

He places the battery in the basket of his bicycle and spots Jason in one of the windows. He wears a pair of swim trunks. A smiling face is painted on his chest. The bass of something modern pounds against the walls, Xavier can feel it in his feet. Jason lights a cigar in his mouth. He piles the dining room chairs by the couch. He flips the coffee table over, knocking bottles to the ground. More furniture collects in the middle of the room. Xavier cruises away.

His Escort is cold and rank. When he opens the hood, flies retreat like freed prisoners. He covers his face with one hand and claws the rotten watermelon from his battery basket. It sticks to his hands, but soon most of it is out. He sits the battery inside, hooks the terminals in place, but without a ratchet or wrench, he only does this much. That's okay, this is a backup plan. He shuts the hood and rolls to Maggie's.

When he climbs into the covers, feels the warmth of her skin against his, he's sorry for what he's just done. It feels unfair of him, but having the option helps him relax. If he never bolts then there's nothing to worry about.

NO CATHARSIS WITHOUT MEMORY

The aquarium in Charlie's pizza joint is filled with hermit crabs. He keeps a few empty shells in there and sometimes the crabs will trade for a few days, hopping homes with inherent indifference. The pizza is decent, but he's transfixed by the presence of Eddie and Wanda, the happy duo. Eddie's hair is neat, shirt tucked in. Wanda laughs with him, offering to buy more pizza if he's hungry. He declines, but takes a set of keys from her and leaves the parlor.

"Kid's a hard-worker," she says. "He could run the place himself if I needed."

Charlie steps from the back. He pulls a couple of pizzas from a brick oven and slices each quickly, tosses a few on a plate for Xavier. "Best breakfast in town."

When Charlie sits, Xavier tells him he might leave.

"And go where? Waldorf?"

Xavier shrugs. "It's home."

Charlie laughs and chomps at the pizza. "Come on, man," he says.

This irks Xavier. He knows why Maryland isn't home anymore, but he wants Charlie to explain it to him. He wants to hear him say that home is with the family, and reason how it is they are still family. Maybe if the thoughts develop aloud, Charlie will exhibit some real remorse.

"I don't think I belong here," Xavier says.

"Nobody belongs in a place they don't stay."

Aubrey stretches and kneads dough at a table. She doesn't seem to have a vision for it. Everything is instinct and thrill. She wears the dough as a mask, rolls it into a snake. She makes gnarled noises. It's all somewhat impish, but Charlie's laughter swamps Xavier.

He finishes his pizza and acquiesces to the laissez-faire temperament. Aubrey's dough behavior is funny when he allows it to be. Xavier joins her at the table. He uses a knife to carve a t-rex. Aubrey studies it, then tears it apart.

After a while, he walks to Maggie's bar. Maggie's flipping through the jukebox and Xavier begins flipping stools. Any qualms circulating within are exorcised by the mindless tasks. He enjoys the procedural opening. When the stools are flipped, he checks that the taps are clean. In the back, he stocks any dishes left to dry the night before. Something jazzy plays from the jukebox. Maggie wipes a few glasses and Xavier pours wine for the each of them. "Today, and today, and today," he says.

The world is quiet.

"I love you," Maggie says.

"I love you, too." He's warm, happy to have no reservations.

A ball-cap donning man with a kickball in hand walks into the bar. Maggie pours him a beer. Xavier sips the wine and enjoys the jazz. The turtles swim unruly.

It's Aubrey's fourth birthday and another storm approaches. Wind pops the balloons tied to the door knob of the pizza joint and the wind whistles in waves. Eddie rolls a tricycle in, dripping with no end. Xavier chews raw pepperonis because Charlie won't serve pizza until the cake arrives. He doesn't have a present. He thinks about his old stuffed t-rex, about Sebastian. Somehow his being here doesn't feel like enough. Maggie taps a keg underneath the gift table. She and Wanda get to filling and Xavier grabs a glass for himself.

When the cake comes Xavier's fuzzed out and the rain's turned sharp. Charlie drops his hand on his shoulder. "I'm glad you're here," he says, and it barely reaches him because conversation has overtaken the parlor.

Xavier cries, but there's no emotional pull, no current receding within that squeezes the tears out. It's closer to a heavy leak and he can't stop so he drinks more. Eddie and Wanda laugh together. Maggie helps cut the cake. Comradery is a word Xavier thinks but doesn't feel. Aubrey peddles the tricycle back and forth because there's nowhere else to go. Behind the counter is a Washington Capitals pint glass—evidence, when one really considered it.

He disappears to take a piss and something dark and weathered floats in the toilet. Xavier uses the plunger to straighten it out and he sees the Salamander's mask, greened by piss and its time underground.

The eye holes stare him out of the bathroom. Back in the front, Aubrey asks him if he's okay. He wants to say something profound but he turns her around instead. She bounces to Charlie.

Outside, the wind whips his hood into his face. His kicks are water logged and the cuffs of his jeans soaked. He passes a swinging payphone and Wanda's shop and makes his way to the Cafeteria.

A wooden fence had been erected around the sinkhole, but now it's broken apart in multiple spots. The storm blows a kickball and one of the hooligans chases it out of sight. All of Xavier is heavy and wet. He sits on the ground, legs crossed. The rain puddles around him and soon it's up to his waist. Streams around the Cafeteria pour water into the sinkhole and for the first time since it formed Xavier can see its bottom. Water creeps up the sides. Trash of different shapes bobs at the surface. He realizes what may bob next and he stands, turns his back to the hole.

Had there been a time portal, Xavier wonders how he would've used it. He's happy to have found Charlie and Aubrey, but the Salamander's death bites at him. The mask on the backdrop of his own piss makes him want to vomit but he didn't drink enough. He imagines Caroline zipping into an asterisk somewhere in his future, a lingering karma. Charlie burned the past too easily.

"Hop in, stupid," Sebastian says.

Xavier searches for him but there's no sign of his Cretaceous friend.

In the distance, somewhere past the Springs, he can see the end of the storm. The gray curls like melted charcoal and cuts to a blue sharper than Sebastian's teeth. It's hard to measure miles in the sky. He wonders how far he'd have to walk to reach the blue. He doubts it would wait for him.

He leaves the Cafeteria.

Back at the party, Maggie pulls him close even though she's dry. He surrenders to her shoulder. Charlie gives a speech about family and how his life hadn't started until he met Aubrey. Xavier drinks some more. He fishes the mask out of the toilet and leaves it in the sink for later.

Xavier walks into the street, craving a cigarette for the first time in weeks, night vision goggles atop his head. He hasn't slept well since Aubrey's birthday. Maggie is sleeping lead and it's too late to bother Charlie. Besides, he's angry. Everything's too easy. He drifts to the convenience store and Malik brushes his teeth using his reflection in the cooler. Down the street someone's installed tetherball and a woman in a sombrero plays alone.

Xavier steps inside and eyes the cigarettes behind the counter. He grabs a carton of chocolate milk instead. "When do you sleep?"

"When you don't see me."

A warm rumble breaks the night and the yellow excavator rolls down the street. Malik raises a pirate sword and lowers it when the excavator passes. "That boy makes me nervous without his brother."

The tetherballer is gone and Xavier follows the heat of the excavator. He pulls the goggles over his head and the world turns grainy and bright. He peeks inside of the bar. The spots where the mop water hasn't dried glow like cigarette burns. The chocolate milk mingles with the stillness of overturned stools, and he wishes the jukebox were playing music unprovoked so he'd have something to work through. Instead, he passes and continues walking until he finds the excavator parked outside the old Rogers saloon. Jason sits in the driver's seat, cigar in mouth, bottle of tequila in his hands. Tied to the machine is a sack of watermelons. He pulls a lever, the thumb extends up and forward and the scooper cuts into the top of the saloon, crushing the ceiling in. Debris drops and splashes in the dirty water of the tank below. The thumb reaches up and over again, and the scooper pulls a larger chunk of roof down. Concrete dribbles out of the scooper and crushes the tank. Glass crashes below and stained water rushes to the street in front of them.

Xavier gulps the chocolate milk and steps to the side of the excavator. Jason swigs the tequila and pukes out the opposite side of the vehicle. "Hey, Batteries Guy. I'm just avenging my own distraught."

Dust from crushed concrete shimmers between them, falling like snow through the night vision goggles. Jason's face mirrors the saloon's collapse. His tears are more familiar than expected. Xavier removes the goggles from his face.

"Your brother's doing alright," he says.

Jason rolls his shiftless eyes. He spits residual vomit out the side and jiggles one of the levers. "Still can't believe Sally's dead," he says.

He raises the thumb and crushes more of the saloon. He drags the scooper, spreading debris across the lot. He repeats. He cries. He swigs. Half of the saloon is crushed.

"Feel better?"

"I'll wake up tomorrow, throned in my own mess and some dudes in matching shirts will clean all this up. Like nothing happened," Jason says.

The nature of consequence has lost its outline for Xavier. He studies the mess of the saloon, the concrete coffin it had been and the pile of rubble it is now. Perhaps physics has its limits, being a set of rules and all. Maybe Newton viewed the world in three dimensions and never accounted for justice—satisfaction, really—as the fourth. What is theory, anyway, if not the result of someone unwilling to take real, concrete action?

Xavier pulls himself into the excavator and Jason slides over. The controls click and jerk and Xavier digs the scooper into another chunk of the saloon, drags it into the street. He repeats until a mound creates a barrier between downtown and the roads to the Springs. From the rubble he pulls a rusted bar and sticks it straight up in the debris, a flagless pole. "Open the sack," he says.

Jason does so and Xavier takes one of the watermelons, impales it with the top of the pole, and slides down until it touches the debris. He does this with a few more melons, until there's room for one more. He hands it to Jason. "This is it. Your monument. You get the one."

Xavier thinks Jason might be too drunk to ride the momentum. He slides on debris as he climbs the mound. His tears and sweat are all one condensation dripping from his jaw to his collar. He holds the watermelon away from his body as if it could drop its teeth in him.

Jason reaches the pole, holds the melon up, and with a good grunt slides it down. He steps away and they admire their industrial fruit kabob. Pieces of the saloon fall and more dust spreads. Jason trots over, takes a piss on the wreckage and returns by Xavier's side.

"Thanks," he says. He climbs into the excavator, starts it up and rolls away from downtown.

No, this won't prove to inspire much consequence, but at the moment, Xavier feels the satisfaction he's been missing. Humidity gets a bad rap, he thinks. Humidity has what they call texture.

Back in the loft, Xavier doesn't go to bed right away. He sifts through Maggie's drawers, finds paper and pen. He scratches away until something similar to Jason's monument comes up. The sketched out watermelons look like tumors without any color and Maggie doesn't seem to have any crayons. He worries Jason might not remember. He worries there's no catharsis without memory.

In the morning, Maggie opens the shop and Xavier is slow to help. The picture is in his pocket, and he'd like to give it to Jason before he proceeds with his day. He hopes to do something worthwhile, to affect this place on a poignant level. Maggie asks him what's wrong, and he tells her he'll be back. The morning is stale. He rides his bicycle toward the demolished saloon, where policemen stand on slabs of concrete, chomping on churros. They stare off in the distance, mindless as goats. Before he makes it much farther, he spots smoke erupting from the Springs. It spins and leans, dark as rotten bark.

When he drops his bike on the sidewalk, the twins' house is already lost. Flames curl out from the windows and smoke blankets the home next door. Xavier doesn't see the excavator anywhere, nor any other sign that Jason is present. He wants to check the windows but even the driveway is out of reach. Instead, he pulls the drawing of the kabob, crumples it, and tosses it towards the house as the policemen pull up, sirens off.

"You do this?" one of them says.

"What are you going to do about it?" Xavier says.

One of them pulls a radio out, calls for a fire truck. The flames reflect in their shades and grow larger. A gust boosts an embered shudder and it flips across the lawn until it crashes into the porch of the neighboring home. It smolders for a bit, smoke peeking from the cracks, before that house catches fire. People file out of their homes, books and computers in hand, children behind them, and evacuate the Springs. It's getting hard to breathe so Xavier pedals away.

He reaches downtown and the melon kabob is glorious in the reddened daylight, smoke dancing behind it. The old saloon looks bombed and a concrete trail leads the eyes to the leaning iron of watermelon. Xavier has to carry his bicycle over the rubble, giving enough time for reminisce, and then he's cruising again. A zipping motor echoes in the distance but no vehicle materializes ahead of him.

The bar seems fragile when he pulls up. Maggie's switched to decaf coffee and she's slow to get things going, so he flips stools and holds her close. "The Springs is on fire," he says.

Maggie seems curious but unconcerned. "Is it bad?"

"Do you have a wrench?"

Maggie rummages through a drawer near the register and hands him a wrench. They walk into the street where people congregate to watch the smoke. Malik is there, the kickballers, the laser taggers. The police join them soon. "That place is done-zo," one of them says, mustache turned upward. He seems excited.

Wanda approaches them with a duffle bag over each arm. She says she's going to Knoxville because she's sick of the flat horizon. "At least in the mountains the creatures will hide," she says. Jason's going to take over her shop until she decides to return. If she decides to return. "What's going on out there?"

"The Springs is on fire."

"Good thing I'm leaving."

People continue to pile into the streets. The sky is tarped, the air is filthy. Charlie carries Aubrey on his shoulders. He stands behind Xavier and Maggie.

"Do you think it will slow?" he says to everyone. Nobody responds, and the smoke thickens. It's difficult to see past downtown. "Where will we go?"

"I tried to help him," Xavier says. "I thought he figured it out."

Eddie pushes past them, polo wrinkled and untucked. "Jason!" he says. He shoves a kickballer to the side, pushes a few other people, until he disappears in the sea of them. Xavier imagines Jason will be waiting for him by the crushed saloon, warmed by the fire. The soot on his face will turn his smile bright. They'll use the excavator and clean the mess together.

Xavier steps to his car, pops the hood. He uses the wrench to tighten the terminals around the battery. He steps into the driver seat and turns the key. It clicks a few times, but the effort is there. He tries one more time. It clicks again and the engine starts. He leaves it on. Exhaust pours from the back and mingles with the rest of the black descending upon them like extra sand poured into an hour glass.

He approaches Charlie, drops his hand on his shoulder. Bits of ash pepper his beard. He smiles and Xavier smiles back. There's a zipping motor behind Charlie, and when Xavier peeks, he doesn't see anything, just a shadow bend around the corner. Aubrey coughs something violent and shields her eyes.

The smoke has reached them. It's a black fog, shielding everything ahead. Xavier's yellow Escort fades little by little into the smoky curtain. Wanda's already disappeared. Maggie grabs his hand. Charlie pulls his khaki cap low.

Xavier watches people fade into black.

Just beyond the smoke, atop of his car, he spots Sebastian, chomping at the wisps that float by. "What are you waiting for?" he says.

SUBLIME

Bad Zeitgeist

As soon as our clothes peeled off, the cart cops pulled up by the river. Carl lay flat on the dock, struggling to button his shirt. Devon and I jumped in naked and huddled near the barnacles, hoping the shadows would shield us from their eyes. We splashed the water and the barnacles slashed us. Carl rolled over and humped up the steps, proving miracles have heartbeats, because I'd never seen a large-backed person right themselves under the direction of a flashlight. He asked the officers for their credentials, and I hid myself in Devon's bosom. Whatever she'd given me, it crushed my sense of situation.

Devon chanted something about regretting an abortion and wrapped her legs around my waist. I was almost hard when something swam beneath us. We floated towards the dock and the moment she and I felt we'd trod to freedom, light fell on our faces. My eyes felt supernova. One security officer demanded our student IDs. His partner asked us why the one guy on land looked like he was drowning.

"Are we in trouble?"

"By the time I wrote the report you'd be eaten by a gator."

The cart cops zoomed around a bush and out of sight and we ran to Tree Hall. The seventh door we tried was unlocked and Carl decided he hadn't had enough to drink for two shenanigans so Devon and I stepped inside and climbed as many steps as we could.

We found a room with a well-placed ladder and too much plastic. Devon peeked in every door, slammed them shut. No sound. Not even a click. A giant window blasted moonlight into this oval den and blood dripped from a barnacle wound in my forearm. The gash looked like a bite mark from a river infant, some aquatic SIDS ghost, bitter of my indifference. Devon had a similarly sticky kneecap, so we danced. Car lights outside passed too quickly, I probably should've missed somebody then, but no one came to mind.

Out the window we saw Carl in the park, on his back again, kicking his shoes off. A slovenly Toyota Camry blew a tire on the bridge, the driver rolled out, and the car tumbled into the river. It hit the water, a creaking dive, and the lights stayed on. A wave smashed onto the park lawn and dampened Carl's shirt, but his snores roared relentless. Too shallow to swallow much, the river buoyed the car with its barnacle barge. The driver sprinted down the street until it looked like her leg snapped at the shin and she tumbled on the asphalt, into street shadows. Carl laughed himself awake.

The plastic on the floor collected the blood from the both of us. Devon did yoga in her panties, took another pill. I counted nails in the wall. Tiny alligators crawled from our wounds and down our legs. They patrolled the red pond rising at our feet. They nibbled at our toes and I missed myself.

Baby, It's Cold Outside

Baylee opens the glass bowl of leftover salad and her left thumb falls off without a mark. It's been numb for a few days, but now it rests atop spinach and grape tomatoes. Italian dressing coats the nail. She picks it up with her other hand. It's knobby and soft, a leather-coated rock. The spot on her hand where it used to sit is closed and scarless. Maybe she never had a left thumb, perhaps a dimensional mirage, but mirages fade, barely leaving a memory. Her thumb rests against a crouton, undoubtedly present. The winter is a little worse this year. It could've frozen off. Baylee's neighbor, a small, cheerful man, says he smells snow on the way. Snow! In North Port!

Roscoe, her husband, made the salad for a special dinner. He does it for himself. A little reminder that she exists, that she's a present member of the household. He's an inventor, so he can check out for a few days at a time. Maybe a few months. It's kind of nice, because Baylee gets to catch up on cheap television and mindless crafts. She's decided to finish her undergrad degree and has completed a few courses over the last year. He stumbles from the office, drunk with guilt, but it's all momentary. He tells her it'll get better, that one invention will satisfy his thirst, but his hibernations are getting longer and longer.

She rinses her thumb and wraps it in foil. She drops it in the freezer, the ice bucket, for preservation. Roscoe's doing a headstand when she walks into the office. "Blood flow to the brain is scientific inspiration," he says.

Baylee waves her hand. Her wedding ring shines brighter without the thumb. "Check this out."

"Carpet that warms your feet," he says to her. "It's getting pretty cold out there."

In their bedroom is a basket of unfolded laundry. She scoops a pair of socks, reaching with her left hand before switching to the right. When she tosses them at her husband he falls over. She studies him while he studies the socks. They stand like that, the Soviet Union and America, until he shuts his eyes and takes a nap. She calls the doctor and makes an appointment.

Her doctor is from Eastern Europe and speaks with an intention that doesn't match his wandering eyes. He wears a fur shawl over his lab coat and tells Baylee the thumb fell off because it lost its utility. "Appendages are an evolving species. There are documented cases of them becoming existential," he says. She can see his breath indoors. He is full fingered, no wedding band present.

"How do I inspire it?"

"Give it a little affection. Perhaps it will crawl back."

When she holds her thumb to her face, it does droop in a familiar way. It's something like slow disappointment, an empty house on Christmas. Baylee asks the doctor for one of his plastic gloves and he lets her have it.

She's left handed and struggles to cut up one of her husband's shirts. She turns the jagged fabric into a small blanket for her thumb. It wiggles in delight but doesn't return to her hand. She rubs it against her cheek, and it rubs her back, but chooses to remain detached. The piece of her husband's shirt isn't warm enough. Cheap cotton fading in a drawer.

Baylee drops the thumb into the appropriate pocket of the doctor's glove and shoves her hand inside before it can jump out. For a moment, it looks whole again, until the thumb thrashes about, its violence pulling the glove off her hand. It looks like it might suffocate, all panic and fear, so she frees it and lets it be for a while.

Over the next few days she doesn't wear any makeup or straighten her hair. She paints the thumb's nail and becomes adept at texting with one hand. Roscoe comes out once to remove a leg from their dining room table and returns to the office. It's his first appearance in weeks. Occasionally Baylee hears their wedding song boom against the walls and she's hopeful. That means he's making progress.

The thumb squirms now. It nestles close, rubs its paddy head against her elbow, but still won't reattach. She tries reading to it, but it only falls asleep. She grabs it and sits it on her hand but it remains independent. Baylee tries super glue, holding the thumb down tight, but it drops to the coffee table and seizes in a way so awful she doesn't try anything else. She resigns to the belief that it'll happen when it happens.

Baylee continues going to classes because it turns out she doesn't really use the thumb when she types. It sits on her desk, thumping and distracting other students. When she raises her hand to answer questions, students murmur to one another. One day, a professor asks her to stay after class. She tells Baylee the same thing happened to her a couple of years ago.

"You shouldn't be so casual about it," she says and holds her hands up. Both thumbs, as well as the left pinky are gone. "Inaction is just as sharp. When I remarried, I started to feel them again, but they never came back." Her face shakes when she says this. Baylee doesn't understand why she bothered remarrying.

The thumb worms about in her pocket. She thanks her professor and considers dropping the class.

Roscoe sits in the living room when she returns from a study session. His face is in his hands and the coffee table is dissembled and lies in pieces. She drops her jacket and scarf over the mess. The thumb sits in her breast pocket. It wiggles and peeks.

She sits next to her husband and rubs his back. He feels like an iceberg.

He turns to her, eyes dry and crusty. His curly hair is flattened by grease. He seems to be looking past Baylee, or at the top of her ear. He takes her hands.

The thumb hops out of her pocket. It crawls down her shirt, down her arm and attaches itself to its rightful place. There's no separation line, as if it never left. It caresses her husband's thumb, rubbing its own prints dull, a ravenous indulgence. For a moment, she can't see the steamy clouds of their breath anymore.

"I'm sorry," he says. "It's another world in there."

There's a tilt from the office, a mechanical gargle, an aluminum stretch.

"I graduate next week. Cap and gown and all," she tells him. "I made reservations at Capono's to celebrate after."

Roscoe hugs her. His breath seeps through the cotton and onto her shoulder. It melts her nerves. His beard cuts through the fabric. "I'm so proud," he says.

The mechanical gargle is louder now. From the hallway comes a robot that can hardly walk. It wobbles like a baby deer, using the table leg as a cane. Its face is made out of their wedding china, its mouth of their Panini press. It opens its mouth and the room's ten degrees warmer. They're both sweating.

The robot reaches forward and beckons Roscoe with its fork fingers.

"Finish me," it says, its voice the grind of a garbage disposal.

Roscoe squeezes her hands. "Next week?" he says.

Baylee nods. Her thumb clamps down like a bear trap.

"Just a few more tweaks. She's almost done." Roscoe stands from the couch, pulls his hand from hers, and joins the robot by the hallway. He pets its face and kisses it on the forehead. Then disappears into the office.

Her thumb doesn't drop off this time. It leaps. It bounces off the couch and onto the carpet. It crawls into the hallway and slips into the office before the door shuts. Her sweat turns to ice, dangles from her ear lobes. Baylee's pinky goes numb. Outside the window, snow falls.

Vertical Leapland

In the last two weeks at Vertical Leapland, fifteen kids have broken a leg. Taylor's boyfriend, Alejandro, shows her the security footage in the back office after work. A kid soars above the trampoline, lands, *snap*. Fifteen times, and only a few of the trampolines are repeat offenders. Vertical Leapland is only six months old and Alejandro worries the trend in vitamin D deficiency will send him into homelessness. Everyone has to sign a waiver prior to jumping, so he's legally protected, but business could thin to a freckle of regulars if it doesn't stop. "I only have a GED and all my Underbelly money went into this." His eyes are restless when he says this. His lip quivering and chapped.

Underbelly used to be the favorite venue for local metal band Team Arson, but a rafter fell on Alejandro during a show, snapping his shoulder, and he sued. Underbelly went under, Alejandro developed a permanent droop on his right side, and he opened up Vertical Leapland after his step-father told him to invest. Crazy part, he pointed out the flimsy rafter a couple shows prior to his accident. It sagged low, water logged by a leak, maybe, but nobody thought anything of it.

Taylor dates Alejandro because he's older and she feels like she's supposed to be doing this kind of thing right now. She's nineteen, has the requisite diploma. He is her boss, twenty-seven, and wears one of those real beards. The kind that burn her lips. Other girls her age have all been with someone five years older at least. Alejandro makes her feel culturally relevant. She hasn't slept with him, yet, nor has he let a loose hand wander. There's a Platonic complacency between them that neither feels compelled to disturb.

After work she buys Vicodin from her old high school English teacher because that's the only way she gets to see her. Mrs. Lawrence (or Carley, as Taylor likes to think, though she never says it aloud) meets her every Tuesday at the lifeguard station that was smashed up by a hurricane. They talk politics, modern literature, and other things of which Taylor pretends to be aware. Seagulls hover too close, overfed by townies. She's had a loitering crush since her days in sophomore English, but hadn't recognized it then. She believes Mrs. Lawrence likes her, maybe in a reciprocal fashion, and Taylor does her best to seem available. She mumbles things like, "You'll have to show me that sometime," and, "Remind me to give you this book I just read," and, "You're too pretty to be married." Mrs. Lawrence's marriage is about as old as Vertical Leapland and Taylor's mind disappears when she mentions her husband, some film he wants to see. "I can get you in for free," Taylor tells her. "It wouldn't be a big deal."

"I'm a little too old for a place like that." Mrs. Lawrence is only twenty-nine and smiles even younger. Her golden hair is shoulder-length and capped with pink highlights. Taylor likes to picture it floating while they bounce on one of the trampolines. Mrs. Lawrence slings Vicodin to help with student loans. "School insurance hooks me up with a liberal doctor," she said. Taylor imagines one night they will split a bottle of gas station wine in Mrs. Lawrence's car before jumping together after hours. Alejandro will be cool because he's old enough to not care about girlfriends anymore.

"It's really for all ages. I've seen parents leave happier than their children," Taylor says. The sun is unrelenting on these afternoons, but she won't let a little burn crush a romantic metamorphosis.

Mrs. Lawrence pockets the cash, tucks a small bag in Taylor's breast pocket. "My husband's cooked a special dinner," she says and waves goodbye.

Taylor lingers long enough to watch her drive away in a door-less jeep. There's a scant creak as the lifeguard stand splinters a little more. The sea gulls drop shits on the soiled wood.

The next week, Juno, lead vocalist of Team Arson, comes in and threatens to burn Vertical Leapland into dead soil. "Nobody will book us," he says. "The magnitude of our metal is a liability." He kicks in the side of the shoe cubby. "You've stolen a commodity from the citizens. I will not tolerate your withholding." He does some of the thrashing he's known to do on stage. The kids around cheer wildly. They jump into each other. When he's gone, suspense shimmers through Vertical Leapland like the final second of a countdown.

Alejandro passes out glasses of milk before he'll open the trampolines to the kids.

"I'm lactose intolerant," says a pale kid wearing a Team Arson t-shirt.

"I'm vegan," says another.

"This is better than the alternative," Alejandro says. He tips the end of the kid's glass to help him finish. "This will help with growing pains."

Soon kids are puking everywhere and they have to close shop for an hour to disinfect. He gives away coupons for buy-one-get-one hours of jumping. Taylor drags a mop across the trampolines while Alejandro stares out the window. There's a van parked across the street. It's spray-painted and big enough to hold a drum set, he says. He's afraid Team Arson means business. Javon, her co-worker, eats pad thai in the ninja course. He wants to help, but all the paranoia makes him hungry. Taylor likes Javon. He's a graphic design major and doesn't take anything too seriously.

Hours later a sophomore from Taylor's alma mater snaps her ankle playing slam ball. She refuses to be carried out until she's finished crying. Alejandro storms into the office, all sweat and shrill. He opens the safe (23-29-31, consecutive prime numbers, he told her) and fingers the cash he's saved up. "Hardly enough," he says. He shuts the safe.

Taylor holds him, kisses his forehead. She tells him to let her try.

Even when she's actively indifferent, Taylor can't ignore a buzzing maternal instinct. She's most attracted to Alejandro when he seems to lose a grip.

In the ninja course, she offers the girl a Vicodin, but only if she comes into the office. Javon carries her in, seats her in a wheeled office chair and Taylor tosses her a water. Alejandro disappears to inspect the springs. He suspects they might be rusted, impugning the elasticity. His mania is intoxicating.

The girl's name is Xyanne and soon she's spinning in the chair, excited to write about the experience in her English journal. "She has us write these prompt-less things and I'm always unsure what to put down. Now I have something to say."

"You have Mrs. Lawrence?"

Xyanne nods, eyes shut. Her ankle is an impressioned peach.

"I think I'm in love with her," Taylor says.

"She's mad fake. Hipster hidden behind crusty novels."

"She's brilliant."

"If you say so." Xyanne stops the spinning. "Wait, did you fuck her?"

Taylor looks out the window. Of course not, she wants to say, nor is she sure she really wants to. Her attraction to Mrs. Lawrence is soft. She'd like to feel their lips graze, the heat of her breath on her neck. Sex feels almost violent, anticlimactic. Before Taylor can say this, Xyanne has hopped out of the office.

By the time they close, the spray painted van hasn't left the other side of the street. Alejandro sits at the computer, eyes glued to the footage from the parking lot camera. He tells Taylor he'll probably stay late and he'll see her tomorrow. When she accidentally hits the light switch on the way out, he doesn't flinch so she leaves it off.

The next few weeks more bones snap but business grows thick. More and more high schoolers want to jump at Vertical Leapland. A young man in cargo shorts dislocates his knee and snags a Vicodin from Taylor. Another kid snaps his shin doing inverted backflips (which are hardly distinguishable from a front flip). He whines enough to grab two Vicodin before he crawls away. Xyanne returns and while she doesn't break anything else, complains that her ankle still throbs from the original incident. Taylor brings her into the office and drops four pills into her palm. She'd like to keep Xyanne close.

After work, Mrs. Lawrence needs to meet somewhere closer to home, so Taylor brings her cash to a bowling alley by the community college. It's loud and dusty.

Mrs. Lawrence dons cheap aviators and a sunhat. Her lips are front and center, her nose thin and acne-scarred. Taylor offers to buy beers. "They never card here," she says. Pins roar behind Mrs. Lawrence. A man in his fifties shoots her a spotted thumbs-up. Mrs. Lawrence says she could kill a few minutes.

Taylor asks about the school year, about her husband, because she wants to feel genuine. She hopes to hear something like regret but marriage is exactly what Mrs. Lawrence wants it to be. Her husband is a freelance app designer, so he stays home or holes up in a Starbucks for a few hours. They have a six-year-old iguana. His pay is irregular, hence the pill dealing, but he is sweet to her. When she comes home, dinner is ready and the DVR is primed. School is rough, because her students seem out of it more and more lately. "I can't get them to think in a logical progression," she says.

"If I were still there I wouldn't be able to take my eyes off you."

To this, Mrs. Lawrence nods her head, takes a swig of her beer.

When the bill comes Taylor realizes she doesn't have enough cash leftover to pay for the Vicodin. Somewhere between romantic impulses she misplaced conventional budgeting. She apologizes, her words clinging to her throat. Her face boils beneath the skin. Looking at the table, she tells Mrs. Lawrence that she can pay her the rest later.

"Just give me what you have and we'll tack it on to next week."

After the bill is paid Taylor has three dollars and change.

Mrs. Lawrence examines the crinkled bills in her palm. Her mouth is shut, lips tight, and through the aviators the rest of her seems frozen. She stuffs the bills into her purse, places a single pill under a napkin. Her unwillingness to soften is devastating. "Have a good rest of your day," she says.

Taylor waits long enough that she won't run into Mrs. Lawrence in the parking lot. The man with the spotted thumb raises his glass, shoots her a wink. "Where'd that beautiful smile go?"

On the phone, Alejandro says he's busy staring at the camera footage again. Juno stopped by with a single stick of dynamite, tossed it to Alejandro and promised there was more to come.

"I swear I saw a lighter flick in the window of the van. I tried to have it towed but there's a certain number of days before--"

Taylor hangs up and heads home.

She steals a bottle of her parent's rum and sips it in her bed. A mist of embarrassment hovers in her room. She sends Mrs. Lawrence a text message. She apologizes for her immaturity and promises it'll never happen again. She blames it on her unconditional affection. She tells Mrs. Lawrence that she'll be here waiting if her marriage fails, or if it doesn't. She reminds her that she's nineteen now, that there's nothing in the way of their being together, and should she ever want to hide away in the ninja course, Taylor would be willing and ready. She tells Mrs. Lawrence that her heart is a spilling well. She quotes Sonnet 18. She tells her next time they meet, she'll be ready to drive away somewhere, to hold nothing back. They could journal it, win the Pulitzer.

Taylor sends the message and sips from the bottle.

The next day a few more teenagers break their legs jumping the trampolines and Alejandro calls in a specialist to inspect the entirety of Vertical Leapland. The specialist is a tiny man with a large wrench and a burgundy jumpsuit. Alejandro directs him between trampolines by waving the stick of dynamite. Taylor hasn't received a response from Mrs. Lawrence.

When the teenagers stop by the office, Taylor tells them she doesn't have any more Vicodin and to make an appointment with their primary care physician. The kids curse and demand she supply them with relief, that they didn't break their legs for nothing, but Taylor can only remind them that she cannot help. A few of them leave, but one girl stays back. Her shin bends about fifty degrees to the right. She wears blue eyeshadow and a Team Arson t-shirt over a sundress. "I know you have to be practical, but if you can't help me, I will die. What's more pragmatic than saving a life?"

Taylor turns her back to the girl, grabs a couple of Excedrin. She drops them into the girl's hand, flashes a wink and Javon steps in to carry her out of Vertical Leapland.

Xyanne floats in after, ankle healed and thin. She's prettier now that she's happy.

"I don't want to lie to you, nor would I prefer to break any more bones," she says.

Taylor pulls the single pill from her purse, but doesn't drop it into Xyanne's hand. "This is my only one, and you have to do me a favor." She rolls herself to the safe, spins the lock, and grabs a few twenties. "Promise you'll give this to Mrs. Lawrence?"

"No doubt," Xyanne says. She takes the cash and the pill and fades out the office. When she's out of sight, Taylor is hopeless.

The specialist doesn't find anything wrong with the trampolines and demands he be paid cash for his trouble. Alejandro slips him a few bills and throws a tantrum when he leaves. He kicks everyone out of Vertical Leapland, and jumps alone for almost an hour. His legs remain whole and narrow. He bares his teeth each time he lands safely.

In his office he watches security footage. "Look at this shit," he says.

Taylor joins him. On the screen, in grainy black and white, is the front parking lot of Vertical Leapland. The spray-painted van sits cold in the distance. A man in a bear costume walks back and forth on all fours. Alejandro fast forwards the tape. The pacing continues for hours. At the end, the bear-man stands up, and over his costume is a large Team Arson t-shirt. He waves a stick of dynamite and walks out of the shot.

Tuesday comes and no word from either Mrs. Lawrence or Xyanne. Alejandro opens Vertical Leapland for limited hours. It reduces the breaks but doesn't stop them from happening. After Taylor turns a few teenagers away consecutively, they stop coming.

She texts Mrs. Lawrence: Usual spot? Maybe if they return to the lifeguard station, things will reset for her.

Hours pass with no response. Alejandro asks if she could watch the floor while he steps out for a bit.

Javon eats curry in the dodgeball cage. Adults in tank tops and bandanas bean each other with the urgency of a guitar riff. Taylor takes a seat next to Javon.

"Maybe it's something in the tap water. Do bones rust?" Javon says. He waves his chopsticks. "This place is incredible. It could be the magnitude of its potential. My bones bend thinking about it."

Taylor scans Vertical Leapland and agrees. It is incredible. She imagines the insides of Mrs. Lawrence to be a similar warmth. Her heart a single trampoline that snaps rule breaking jumpers. Her mind a dodgeball cage. Her vagina a ninja course.

She sends another message: I'm free anytime. Probably not doing anything later.

When Alejandro returns he's slung a crossbow over his shoulder and carries a case of energy drinks. He pulls one of the wheeled office chairs to the parking lot where he stations himself for the night. The crossbow rests in his lap and he keeps his face turned toward the spray-painted van.

Taylor watches him through the security footage until they close up shop. He only breaks to piss in the trees nearby. She still hasn't heard from Mrs. Lawrence. On her way out, Alejandro doesn't acknowledge her. A thin mutt sniffs the door of the van and barks a few times before trotting after a cyclist.

Her alma mater is a neighborhood school and she remembers that she would spot Mrs. Lawrence walking home during lacrosse practice. She would take a right out the school and then a left at Seaweed Street.

The detour isn't too out of the way. If Taylor makes her way towards Seaweed Street then all she has to do is take Sixth down to Pablo and her home is a straight shot from there.

The last time she and Alejandro ate a meal together, she spent most of the evening mulling the idea for a film. Alejandro scooped something rice related onto a plastic plate and she invented a character named Gabriella. Gabriella was sweet, overly empathetic, and hungry to become a vet even though she feared blood. Her favorite color was aqua, her favorite book *Emma*. Her movie begins with a Florida panther on the side of I-95.

Alejandro put on a real film, something Tarentino, and Taylor built a resentment for Gabriella. Not because she couldn't see the rest of her story, but because it was incredibly easy to. Gabriella had a goal, a real desire, and as that desire took shape in Taylor's mind, she found herself finding Gabriella less and less familiar.

Taylor watched Alejandro shovel food into his mouth. The light of the television carved shadows around his moving jaw, giving shape to his contentment.

"Anything else you want?" Alejandro said, his shoulder with an extra slump.

"I don't think so."

Seaweed is a shaded street. It's dark and the windows glow yellow. Moss hangs low and trash cans await the morning pick-up. Basketball hoops dot cul-de-sacs, shingles ice roofs.

A man in a ball cap and pajamas walks a drooping iguana in the middle of the street. He waves at Taylor and asks her for a light. "The wife threw mine out and this is my only chance to smoke."

She tells him no and the man shrugs, disappointed. He's rugged, athletic, and handsome enough, despite the break in his nose. She gets another idea. "Do you want to go somewhere?"

"What do you mean?"

She steps a little closer, presses her chest out, gives her eyes a deliberate laziness. She imagines the humidity awards her a gloomy kind of glisten. "There's this trampoline place if you want to bounce around."

The iguana hisses.

"The fuck is wrong with you?" The man pulls the leash and walks the iguana away, around a corner past a stumpy palmetto.

Soon she's alone and her phone buzzes: I can find you a new dealer if you want.

She replies: I'm in the neighborhood, can we talk?

Taylor follows the path of the iguana. A couple of teenage boys in Team Arson t-shirts cruise by on long boards, one of them shoots her a middle finger, the other mimes masturbation. The stumpy palmetto rustles in the night. Around the corner she finds Mrs. Lawrence's doorless jeep. When she reaches it, she slips into the passenger seat. Through a small window near the front door, Taylor spots Mrs. Lawrence at the dining room table, sifting through a stack of papers.

She sends another message: We can meet at the stumpy palmetto.

Mrs. Lawrence grabs her phone from the table, reads it, and peeks out the window.

Taylor ducks in the seat. Her hand finds itself in the front of her pants. She waits to be discovered and massages herself, soft at first, then more deliberate. She thinks about Mrs. Lawrence circling something on the paper, and moves her fingers in a similar fashion. Maybe if she's caught, Mrs. Lawrence will understand, will drive them somewhere more private. She imagines hiding in the ninja course. There's a magnetism bouncing from her chest, something indicative of subterranean potential. Something worth planting a flag in.

Her phone buzzes: Go home, Taylor. I will call the police.

Taylor scoots herself up and catches Mrs. Lawrence reading one of the papers. Her husband comes from a hallway, glass of wine in hand and sets it on the table. They kiss, and Mrs. Lawrence holds his face. He smiles.

Taylor slips out the jeep, her hand out of her pants. She turns her phone off and leaves the neighborhood.

Alejandro is on his feet, crossbow raised, when she returns to Vertical Leapland. He tip-toes across the parking lot towards the street.

"Come out! I saw you!"

He fires an arrow into the side of the van. It whistles and it thumps.

Taylor walks to his side and Alejandro reloads the cross bow. She asks him what he sees.

"That bear-man was thrashing about back there." He raises the crossbow, fires another into the side of the van.

The shirted bear-man dashes from behind the van and sprints down the street. Alejandro fumbles with an arrow and the bear-man is gone before he can reload, a consequence of his drooping shoulder. "Shit!" he says.

They cross the street together. Taylor's gloss has turned into a sweat. She wishes it would rain.

Up close she can see how erratic and uneven the van's paint job is. It looks honey gold in the street light. The arrow punctures curve in and tight like a steel belly button. Alejandro pulls but they won't budge. A breeze whips through and they get a whiff of something fruity and rancid. It feels like poison in Taylor's sinus cavity.

Alejandro says it's coming from the car. No one's in the driver's seat so they pull on the handle of the side door. It's unlocked.

The door slides open, and sitting up, leaning against the back window is a rank smelling man. He dons a Team Arson t-shirt and a rubber hose around his elbow. His skin is see-through and his mouth is rigored upward at the corners.

Taylor can't watch for too long before she feels sick. She steps away and crosses the street. She turns her phone on. There's a new message: I think it's best this way.

Down the street, Juno marches forward, torch in hand. Behind him is a group of teenagers, all covered in Team Arson t-shirts. Some of them gallop on crutches, others wheel themselves forward in chairs. There might be a chant, but all Taylor can hear is the sharp hiss of the iguana echo in her memory.

Alejandro grabs her hand. He pulls her close. He's as warm as her pockets. "Are you okay?" he says.

Taylor bites his shirt, and while she doesn't say a thing, knows that she isn't.

The Matter of Dust

The Sheep

My neighbor shears a sheep in his driveway. The sheep is on its back, and he stands directly over it, starting with the belly. The strokes are deliberate, like steam-cleaning the carpet, or swimming Olympic laps. In Florida it doesn't snow, but sometimes I have to wear a jacket, which I am, and smoke a cigarillo because it makes me feel warmer. I used to drink when I was cold, but that became when I was tired, or when I was happy, or when I was doing the laundry.

Shearing in the winter, I don't understand it.

There's no farm nearby. The HOA fees here are high. I wonder if the sheep is a pet.

A thin breeze whips smoke from my cigarillo into my neighbor's driveway. Balls of gray… fur? lint? stuffing? fall onto my neighbor's arm, smoothing the dark of his wrist hair. The sheep baas when it tastes my smoke.

"Do you mind? That kills," my neighbor says. He pauses the shave, and the sheep is half-full. Its tongue sits limp on the side of its mouth, its eyes are mindless. "Appreciate it."

I don't want to go inside because there are three urns awaiting me. Something's to be done with each of them, and urns don't come with instructions; at least not the kind I need.

"Want to give it a go?" my neighbor says. He's yet to continue, and despite the cold he rubs sweat from his forehead, pulls a beer from a small cooler. I'd like to give it a go, touch the bottom of our bottles together, maybe tell him about the ash. Maybe he already knows.

I sit on the sleeper-sofa in my garage. Close my eyes. The cigarillo stills burns in my hands, proves to be a hazard. My breathing slows.

The Urns

What's that game called, where you hide a ball under one of three cups, and switch them around, hoping to confuse the audience? They play it at the Jumbo Shrimp games here.

One urn should be my father, the other my mother, and the third my paraplegic cousin Ross. The truth is, neither has an identifying mark on it, and it wouldn't matter if they did. The ashes inside are a potpourri of them, the house, and a woodland creature or two. Scooped from the remains of a fire. The three separate urns are all gesture.

This might be why I don't know what to do with them.

They sit in a triangle in my lanai, sixty degrees between the three of them. When I hold them individually, they feel the same weight, but I imagine they might be a pound or two different.

I'm afraid to spread them at the beach because a seagull might fly through them, dirtied until it rained.

I'm afraid to bury them because of what might grow. For whatever reason, I envision a potato vine, familiar faces constructed by dirt and bruising.

I'm afraid to hold on to them, place them on the mantel, because this house has brand new carpet, and the vacuum cleaner is too good not to use. I will get drunk and knock them over. I almost want to.

There's a smell to them. I know this because the lanai used to smell like outside, the humid nest of insects. Now it smells like Johnny Walker, my memory of it.

The Fire

It was probably arson. The fire originated in a home of heritage; built by uncompensated labor and abandoned for the tax-free wealth of another country. Neighbors believe it was the bitter, unrewarded son. The one they left behind. An eye witness claims a blazing shudder flipped from the first house, hit my parents' porch, and thus began the spread.

The entire neighborhood was grounded. Buildings were stained with ash and now their downtown looks beautifully ombréd. That's what they say.

My parents were asleep. Ross couldn't crawl fast enough.

This House

Inheritance casually carries a positive connotation. It's almost synonymous with "gift" though it rings with more entitlement.

Investment property, my father had said.

Rent this place out, my mother had said. Save it for grandchildren.

Ross didn't have choice. I wasn't going to take care of him. He had to leave with them.

Most of my furniture is still in the garage. I only use the kitchen and the bathroom. My parents haven't – hadn't – lived here in about seven years. They had loyal renters, but I'm still afraid of the musk of absence.

I don't know why they moved, other than they wanted the air to taste different.

The Clippers

I'm outside again. Smoking another cigarillo, because I can't sleep this early, another occasion to drink.

The sheep baas and lips the rope tied around its neck. It's still only half-shaved. My neighbor's Toyota is out of sight.

When I stand next to it, the sheep hardly registers my presence.

Leftover fur? lint? stuffing? surrounds the legs. I consider pressing my cigarillo into them, watching it smolder like a battery to steel wool.

Wool.

Underneath the chair are the clippers, still plugged into an extension cord. I flip them on and the sheep flinches, wrinkles its lip. I grab the clippers, straddle the animal as if I were to ride it, and run them along its back. I repeat until the sheep is almost fully shaved. Men shear sheep to prevent their overheating, to avoid any decrease in their mobility. How does one herd when all around him is drag?

There's a pleasure in the trim, like scissors to construction paper, but I can't decipher the sheep's baas. Is it pleasurable, like scratching an itch? Does it hurt? Does it burn?

I drop the clippers. They rattle against the concrete like a fallen moth.

I untie the sheep. There's no morality here, I just want to see it move, wonder how it will choose which way to go.

When the rope drops, the sheep is still. But I'm not. I scoop the fallen wool, the remains, and cross the street.

The Attic

Renters don't use the attic. That's what I've heard. I've also heard it's where ghosts live.

When I climb the ladder, I find old boxes from my childhood. Holiday decorations. Little League jerseys. Looney Tune kites. In the corner, I find an ottoman. Inside the ottoman are old Polaroids. White frames from the 90s. The pictures are glued together with neglect. Roaches leap from the cardboard flaps. Is this what dust is made of?

I remove the photographs and stuff the ottoman with the sheep's wool. It takes me two trips, but I carry the urns in there as well. I pour the ashes onto the wool. They settle like spilled wine. The back of my throat itches, the grooves of my spine tickle with sweat. Everything is ingredients.

When I'm out of the attic, the baa of the sheep shakes me. It stands in my driveway, lips pulled by gravity. I drag the sleeper sofa into the living room. I hang some clothes in the closet.

Notes and Acknowledgments

Thank you to the journals that gave these stories their first home and took a chance on a guy writing some weird things, including:

"Sinking Moments" - Flock
"An Unfaded Black" - Oyster River Pages
"Goose Island" - Panhandler Magazine
"Unsolicited Independence" - Yellow Chair Review
"Scoop Carry Dump Repeat" - Saw Palm
"Cages" - Hobart
"Gastropod" - Eyeshot
"Terra" - Literary Orphans
"The Sinkhole" – Fjords Review
"Bad Zeitgeist" - The Molotov Cocktail
"Baby, It's Cold Outside" - Atlas and Alice
"Vertical Leapland" - Carbon Culture Review
"The Matter of Dust" - Split Lip Magazine

Thank you to the various readers and mentors along the way, including Jeff Parker, Jason Ockert, Jessica Anthony, Corinna Vallianatos, and Kevin Moffett. Whether in the classroom, through email, or over foosball at the Hub, your insight into my writing has been invaluable. Thank you for being the best, and thank you Erica Dawson for leading such a strong and supportive program at the University of Tampa.

Thank you to everyone at Barrelhouse. Between accepting me as part of the literary community to reading my work at Writer's Camp, you've allowed me to believe that maybe I belong in this world.

Thank you, Jared Rypkema and the rest of Bridge Eight. I love our press and the work we're doing in Jacksonville.

Forever thanks to the staff at Pride Rock Bar, aka #TeamVisc, aka Mike Weber, Grace Lanoue, Riley Manning, and C.H. Hooks—may Urban Cantina never run out of chips.

Thank you to my family, who may not read this book, but are on my mind every time I write.

And thank you to my wife, Brittany. I don't deserve you, but I'm working really hard to make up for that.

MASTODON TITLES

FICTION

Life During Wartime by Katie Rogin
A Diet of Worms by Erik Rasmussen
The Pleasures of Queueing by Erik Martiny

SHORT FICTION

Dead Aquarium by Caleb Michael Sarvis

YOUNG ADULT

Fear to Shred by Joan Gellfend

MEMOIR

Gatsby's Child by Dorin Schumacher

POETRY

Give a Girl Chaos by Heidi Seaborn

SPECIALTY

Manson Family Paper Doll Book by John Reed